SCREAM STREET

Book Thirteen

FLAME OF THE DRAGON

The fiendish fun continues at
www.screamstreet.com

SCREAM STREET

Book Thirteen
FLAME OF THE DRAGON

TOMMY D☠NBAVAND

CANDLEWICK PRESS

Text copyright © 2011 by Tommy Donbavand
Illustrations copyright © 2011 Cartoon Saloon Ltd

First U.S. edition 2015

Library of Congress Catalog Card Number 2014954529
ISBN 978-0-7636-5765-9

15 16 17 18 19 20 FRS 10 9 8 7 6 5 4 3 2 1

Printed in Altona, Manitoba, Canada

This book was typeset in Bembo Educational.
The illustrations were done in ink.

Candlewick Press
99 Dover Street
Somerville, Massachusetts 02144

visit us at www.candlewick.com

For me!
(Well, I wrote them all!)

Meet the residents

Luke Watson

Cleo Farr

Resus Negative

Dixon

Sir Otto Sneer

Samuel Skipstone

Alston and Bella Negative

Eefa Everwell

Doug

Dr. Skully

Niles Farr

Mr. and Mrs. Watson

Who lives where

- **A** Sheer Hall
- **B** Central Square
- **C** Everwell's Emporium
- **D** No. 2: The Crudleys
- **E** No. 5: The Movers
- **F** No. 11: Twinkle

- **G** No. 13: Luke Watson
- **H** No. 14: Resus Negative
- **I** No. 21: Eefa Everwell
- **J** No. 22: Cleo Farr
- **K** No. 26: The Headless Horseman

- **L** No. 27: Femur Ribs
- **M** No. 28: Doug, Turf, and Berry
- **N** No. 31: Kian Negative
- **O** No. 32: Ryan Aire
- **P** No. 39: The Skullys

When Luke Watson first began to transform into a werewolf, his whole world was turned upside down—especially when his family was forcibly moved to a new home on Scream Street. This secure, magically locked location was one of several communities in which G.H.O.U.L. (Government Housing Of Unusual Life-forms) placed vampires, witches, zombies, and more.

Luke quickly made friends with the wannabe vampire next door, Resus Negative, and Cleo Farr, a plucky mummy from down the street—but his parents were terrified. So with the help of his new friends, he set out to collect six relics left behind by the community's founding fathers. Only with their combined power could he open a doorway back home, even though such portals are against the rules. However, by the time Luke had succeeded, his parents had seen how happy he was on Scream Street and decided to stay.

Meanwhile, doorways work in both directions, and it wasn't long before Scream Street's greedy landlord, Sir Otto Sneer, was charging "normals" from Luke's old world to visit what he called "the world's greatest freak show." Soon the street was swarming with tourists, making life a misery for the residents.

This set Luke, Resus, and Cleo off on a second quest: to track down the founding fathers and return their relics in an effort to close the doorway and save their friends and neighbors. Five relics in, all seemed to be going well — until the illegal doorway was discovered and the trio was caught by Acrid Belcher, the disgusting swamp beast head of G.H.O.U.L. . . .

The Punishment

Mr. and Mrs. Watson gripped the bars of the viewing area as they watched the Movers march Luke, Resus, and Cleo over to the trapdoor. Niles Farr and Resus's mom and dad were with them. The trip through the Hex Hatch to G.H.O.U.L. headquarters had been made in silence, apart from the occasional sob from Bella Negative.

The trio had their hands tied and they stood, staring miserably at their parents as Acrid Belcher approached, clutching a roll of parchment. Cleo began to shake. Resus fought back tears as he caught sight of his mom's stricken face.

"Defendants," the slime beast gurgled. "You have been charged with opening a magical doorway out of a G.H.O.U.L. community, allowing thousands of normals to enter and disrupt the lives of its residents. Do you deny these charges?"

"You don't understand," protested Luke. "I just wanted a way to take my mom and dad home. . . ."

"Then you admit to collecting the six founding fathers' relics and using their power to open a doorway back to your old world?"

"Yes, but—"

"Enough!" barked Belcher. "You are guilty of the charges brought against you, and sentence will now be passed."

Luke gulped and didn't say any more.

"Luke Watson, Resus Negative, Cleo Farr— you will now be banished to the Underlands for the rest of your natural lives, however long that may be."

Acrid Belcher grasped the lever beside him and pulled it back hard. The trapdoor swung open with a barely audible creak, plunging Luke, Resus, and Cleo into the dark, swirling abyss beneath. . . .

Chapter One
The Underlands

As Luke tumbled through the purple clouds, he found himself in the middle of a violent storm. He could just make out the desolate features below: black soil, twisted trees, and a raging river of churning, dark water.

Then he caught sight of Resus and Cleo, also midfall, being buffeted by the wind as the ground sped toward them. Luke felt consumed with guilt. This was all his fault. His friends hadn't been in any danger until he had involved them in his quest to find the founding fathers' relics. "I'M SORRY!" he bellowed.

Cleo managed to flash him a quick smile before a crackling bolt of purple lightning shot between them, sending her spiraling backward. Resus grabbed the mummy's foot before she could disappear into the sheets of torrential rain, pulling her toward him so that Luke could catch her other hand.

"HOLD ON!" shouted the vampire, then he plunged his hand into his cape and pulled out a large golf umbrella, forcing it open against the howling wind. Instantly, the trio's descent slowed as the umbrella acted like a parachute. They were still falling, but the ground wasn't rushing up to meet them quite so quickly. Maybe they could survive this fall after all. . . .

"YOU'RE A GENIUS!" cried Luke.

"*FINALLY* YOU REALIZE!" Resus grinned. "AFTER ALL—"

His words were cut off abruptly as another fork of fiery lightning arced toward them, slamming into the handle of the umbrella with the force of a charging bull. Both vampire and umbrella were flung away across the sky in a blaze of fizzing violet sparks.

"RESUS!" screamed Cleo.

Luke twisted around, trying to spot a flash of the blue lining of his friend's cape among the pounding sheets of gray rain, but there was nothing. Resus was gone.

Then Luke plunged into the heaving waters of the river, and pain exploded in his knee as it smashed against a rock.

The freezing water bit at Luke. He opened his eyes but could see nothing in the inky blackness. The river spun him around and around, and he could feel his lungs burning. He needed to work out which way was up and get to the surface so he could breathe again—but he had lost all sense of direction in the turbulent water.

The pain in his knee began to overwhelm him and he found himself thinking about his mom and dad. He'd started searching for Scream Street's hidden relics as a way to take his parents back to their old world. They hadn't asked to be moved—it had all been because he had started transforming into his werewolf. Now he would never see them again. A veil of unconsciousness began to wash over him. . . .

Then, suddenly, a hand plunged into the water, grabbed the collar of his T-shirt, and dragged him to the surface. Luke gulped down a lungful of freezing air.

"I'm not losing you, too!" gasped Cleo as she pumped her legs to try to keep the two of them afloat. Lashing rain hammered down all around them like needles. "Can you swim to the river-bank?" she shouted.

Luke shook his head. "I hit my leg," he replied weakly.

Gritting her teeth, Cleo wrapped her arm around Luke's chest and began to swim toward the bank. A deep red stain spread out behind them in the water as blood gushed from Luke's injured knee.

Finally, Cleo found she was able to stand. Her legs tired and shaking from the cold, she dragged Luke clear of the water, then slumped to the ground beside him. As the pair struggled to catch

 5

their breath, the charred remnant of the umbrella handle was whipped out of the sky and embedded itself in the mud next to them.

"Resus!" croaked Luke. Then the world went black.

When Luke opened his eyes again, the rain had stopped—although dense, plum-colored clouds still rolled across the sky and a strong breeze made him shiver in his wet clothes. Cleo was kneeling beside him, wrapping a length of her own bandages around his injured knee.

"How does it look?" he asked, trying unsuccessfully to ignore the pain.

Cleo tied the makeshift dressing in place. "Pretty bad," she said. "It's bleeding quite heavily. I think it'll need stitches."

"Not much chance of that here," said Luke glumly.

"No," Cleo agreed. "Think you can stand?"

"I'll give it a try. . . ."

Cleo grabbed Luke's arm and helped him to his feet. He took a tentative step, but the pain exploded in his knee and he fell back to the ground.

 6

"Get me that stick," he said through gritted teeth, pointing to a blackened branch that had been washed up by the river.

Cleo retrieved the branch and handed it over. Luke plunged one end into the soft, wet mud and used it to drag himself upright. "There!" He smiled, wedging it under his arm. "I can use this as a crutch. Come on, we need to find Resus."

But before he could take a step, an unexpected noise reached him—the sound of wet, ragged breathing. He froze.

"Behind you . . ." Cleo warned.

Luke turned to find a huge troll lumbering toward them, teeth bared. "Stay back!" Luke cried.

The troll grunted and took another step toward them.

"I'm warning you!" Luke declared, sounding braver than he felt. "I'm a werewolf, and I'm prepared to attack."

Still the troll kept coming.

Luke tossed the stick aside, closed his eyes, and tried to trigger his werewolf transformation. He felt the rage begin to build at the back of his mind and he held his muscles taut, ready to be reshaped.

The troll was almost upon them now.

"Any time you like . . ." hissed Cleo, struggling to keep the panic out of her voice.

Luke opened his eyes again. "I can't transform," he breathed. "I'm just too exhausted. Sorry . . ."

Before Cleo could reply, the troll grabbed both children and held them up to its face. "You two are comin' wiv me!" it growled.

Chapter Two
The Village

The Underlands flashed by as the troll
ran through sparse woodlands and bleak fields,
Cleo tucked under one arm and Luke under the
other.

If the mummy wasn't being bounced up and down with every footfall, she would have commented to Luke how similar this journey was to the one they'd endured the last time they'd been snatched by trolls. "I think I'm going to be sick!" she groaned. Luke didn't reply; his knee was still bleeding badly and his eyes were heavy.

Cleo knew she had to do something. Last time they had almost been cooked alive, only managing to save themselves by setting off some fireworks Resus had found in his cape. But now Resus wasn't here, and Luke looked as if he might pass out at any second. It was up to her.

Closing her eyes tightly, Cleo stretched down and bit the troll as hard as she could on the bottom. The creature let out a howl, flung the pair to the ground and began to hop around in circles, clutching his backside.

"What did ya bite me for?" he wailed.

"I decided that if one of us was going to be eaten, it wouldn't be me!" replied Cleo, licking her lips and doing her best to look wild-eyed and crazy.

"I wasn't gonna eat you!" grunted the troll, offended.

"Of course not," said Cleo sarcastically.

 10

"I was tryin' to help you!" insisted the troll.

"Help us?"

The troll nodded. "Your friend's hurt his leg, so I reckoned I'd better take you to . . ." He stopped and leaned closer, peering at Cleo's face. "'Ere, I know you. . . ."

"You do?" said Cleo, taken aback.

The troll looked over at Luke, then back at Cleo. "You was in the cage wiv me all them weeks ago. You helped me find my friend!"

Cleo felt her anger drain away. The creature was right! She, Luke, and Resus had been locked in a holding cell at G.H.O.U.L. headquarters after they'd accidentally become trapped outside Scream Street, and the troll had been there too.

"You're Wompom!" said Cleo, suddenly remembering.

"That's right." The troll beamed, snatching her up and giving her a hug. "We saw some kids drop through the trapdoor from G.H.O.U.L., so I came runnin' as quick as I could to see if you was OK."

"Who's 'we'?" asked Cleo.

Wompom smiled. "Just you wait an' see. . . ."

It took another hour to reach the village. Cleo, who was now sitting astride Wompom's shoulders, stared open-mouthed at the collection of ramshackle huts inside a barbed-wire fence.

A rough sign proclaimed:

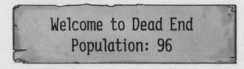

Welcome to Dead End
Population: 96

"Dead End?" said the mummy.

Wompom carefully lowered Luke to the ground and lifted Cleo off his shoulders. "Your new home," he announced proudly. "It's not much, but we like it."

"You keep saying 'we,'" Cleo pointed out. "Do you mean you and your wasp friend?"

"Lan's here," said Wompom, "but not just him. The people what live in Dead End are them who's been banished to the Underlands by G.H.O.U.L."

"Criminals!" exclaimed Cleo.

"Not anymore," Wompom assured her. "Some of 'em did some naughty things in the past, but now we all work together to make the best of whats we've got."

"What's going on?" slurred Luke, coming around. "Where are we?"

"Your friend's lost a lot of blood," Wompom told Cleo, picking Luke up again. "Lan will know what to do wiv him. Come on."

"Halt!" came a voice as they reached a small wooden gate. "Who goes there?" Piercing green eyes glared at the group through a slot cut into the gate.

"It's me, Wompom," replied the troll.

"I can see that, you idiot!" snapped the voice. "Who's this you've got with you?"

"The kids wot fell down from G.H.O.U.L.," said Wompom. "I've brought 'em back. One of 'em's hurt."

"How do you know we can trust them?"

The troll scowled. "Rooney—you was sent 'ere for robbin' anyone wot tried to get a peek at your pot of gold. I'd trust a fartin' goblin quicker than I'd trust you! Now, open this gate afore I rip it off its hinges and feed it to you."

"All right, all right," grumbled the voice. The gate swung open and Cleo was surprised to see the figure behind it jump down from a wooden

crate. He was a tiny man, dressed in an emerald suit and sporting a mop of shocking red hair.

"Rooney's the most wanted leprechaun in the world," Wompom whispered to her. "Or he was until they caught him trying to sell fake rainbows to tourists. . . ."

"That's enough talk!" snapped Rooney, slamming the gate shut behind them. "Now, off to the hospital before I change my mind."

"Hospital" turned out to be a rather grand title. Wompom led Cleo past several tumbledown shacks and into a cabin made of corrugated iron. Inside were two beds, one of them shrouded by a dirty, torn curtain. The troll laid Luke on the other.

Cleo took Luke's hand and held it tightly. His injured leg was caked in dried blood, and he was beginning to sweat.

The door opened again and a giant wasp flew in, wings buzzing noisily. "Where isss the new arrival?" he hissed.

"On the bed," said Wompom. "He's hurt his leg."

Lan Mossdrop landed beside Luke's bed and folded his wings against his back.

"Can you help him?" Cleo asked.

14

"We are not blessssssed with the latessst equip-
ment," Lan replied, "but I promissse to do my
bessst." He pulled back Luke's torn jeans and
began to examine the wound. "Thisss will require
ssstitchesss," he announced, and with that he
turned his back and began to sew up the gash,
using his own stinger as a needle.

"Lan looks after everyone who gets sick here
in Dead End," said Wompom proudly. "He did a
great job fixin' up that other kid."

If Cleo's heart hadn't been safely stored away
in a fridge back on Scream Street, it would have
skipped a beat at this news. "What other kid?"
she asked cautiously.

"This one," said Wompom, pulling aside the
dirty curtain around the second bed. Cleo's face
fell. Instead of the vampire she had been hoping
to see, a young skeleton lay there, just waking up.

"What's wrong?" asked Wompom.

"Nothing." The mummy sighed. "I just
thought it might be our friend."

The skeleton had other ideas, however. He
leaped out of the bed and threw his bony arms
around Cleo. "You're alive!" he exclaimed. "I
thought I'd never see you again!"

 15

Cleo untangled herself from the skeleton's grip and took a step back. "I'm sorry," she said indignantly, "do I know you?"

"Of course you do!" beamed the skeleton. "It's me—Resus!"

Chapter Three

The Crowd

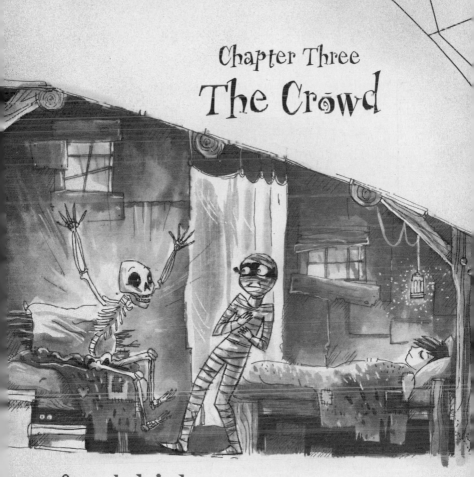

Once Luke's leg had been stitched up, Lan buzzed out of the room.

"Your friend will have to rest now," Wompom told Cleo, "but you can stay with him until he wakes up. We'll be back to check on him later."

As soon as the door closed behind the pair, Cleo turned to face the skeleton. "I don't know who you are, but you're certainly not Resus," she said firmly.

"Of course I'm Resus!" insisted the skeleton. "Look, I've got this to prove it." He reached under his pillow and pulled out a vampire cape with a blue lining.

"Where did you get that?" demanded Cleo, snatching the cape from him. "This belongs to our friend."

"It *does* belong to your friend," hissed the skeleton. "Me!" He closed his eyes and there was a sound like a bath being emptied. His bones began to ripple and change shape, and within seconds he had turned into a very familiar vampire.

"It *is* you!" cried Cleo in amazement.

Resus looked over at the other bed. "What's wrong with Luke?"

"He cut his leg when he landed," Cleo replied. "What happened to you?"

"I landed in a tree not far from here," Resus told her. "I've got a few bruises, but nothing more."

"Nothing more?" cried Cleo. "You were a skeleton just now!"

Resus grinned. "I was, wasn't I!"

"But . . . *how*?"

"With a bit of help," said Resus. "Look under the bed. . . ."

Cleo crouched down and peered into the gloom beneath the rusty frame—to see her own reflection looking back at her in a pair of familiar mirrored sunglasses. "Zeal Chillchase!" she exclaimed.

The Tracker raised a finger to his lips, then indicated a loose panel in the wall just behind him. He pushed it aside and crawled through.

Cleo glanced back into the room. "Can we leave Luke?"

"He'll be OK for a minute," Resus whispered. "Come outside where we can talk."

The pair crawled under the bed after the Tracker and out through the makeshift exit. They found Chillchase waiting for them at the back of the hospital shack.

"Acrid Belcher *told* us he'd sent you here, too!" cried Cleo.

"He did," said Zeal. "Obviously not long before you. I was just searching for a place to make camp when I found Resus hanging out of a tree."

"Mr. Chillchase brought me here to get checked out," Resus added.

"But why all the secrecy?" asked Cleo. "Why were you hiding under the bed?"

Zeal pulled off his mirrored sunglasses. "I was the one who condemned most of the residents of Dead End to the Underlands," he explained. "I don't think they'd be too happy to see me again."

"Then why not shapeshift into someone they don't recognize?"

"My power is almost completely drained," said Zeal. "Acrid Belcher made sure of that. If I draw upon my reserves, I might have *just* enough left to open a Hex Hatch out of this terrible place."

"Can we really escape from the Underlands a second time?" asked Cleo.

"We have to," said Resus. "We have to save everyone at home. There's just one more relic to return and then we can close that doorway forever."

"I can't believe Belcher's working with Sir Otto now," said Cleo. When the head of G.H.O.U.L. had found out that Scream Street's landlord was charging tourists to visit the street, he had allowed him to continue in return for a cut of the profits.

"I've always had my suspicions about Acrid

Belcher," said Chillchase. "But I never thought he'd go this far."

"Zeal helped me shapeshift so that I won't be recognized when we get back to Scream Street," Resus told Cleo proudly. "That's how I became a skeleton."

"But how?" Cleo asked the Tracker. "You said you hardly had any power left."

"Gutweed," explained Chillchase. "It contains the same chemicals that shapeshifters have naturally inside them. Eating it can mask your true identity for short periods of time."

"*Eurgh!*" said Cleo, pulling a face. "You mean the stuff that grows in sewers?"

Chillchase nodded. "I keep a small supply in my boots in case of emergencies."

Now it was Resus's turn to make a face. "You might have said that before I ate the stuff! I didn't think—"

"Well, well, what have we here?" a shrill voice interrupted. Zeal and the children looked up to see Rooney the leprechaun coming over. "Here's me on my way home after a long shift on the gate, and who do I find but the very fellow who sent me here?"

"I don't want any trouble, Rooney," said Chillchase.

"That's a shame," snarled the leprechaun. "'Cos trouble's the one thing we've got plenty of around here." He stuck two fingers in his mouth and whistled loudly. "Hey, lads—would you come and look at this!"

Shack doors began to open all over Dead End, and the angry

faces of ogres, zombies, and demons peered out. What appeared to be an exceptionally large lizard slithered over to join the leprechaun. "Ith that who I think it ith?" the creature lisped.

Rooney cracked his knuckles. "It most certainly is, Higgs!"

"What is *that*?" whispered Cleo.

"A lamia," replied Chillchase. "I banished him here for smuggling zombie parts over to Hollywood to be used as movie props."

The lizard creature whipped its tail angrily from side to side as it slid closer. "I have a thcore to thettle with you, Chillchathe!"

"So do I!" barked an orc. "I had a nice little sideline in illegal weapons till he busted me."

"He sent me here for kidnappin' an elf," snarled an ogre.

The mood was getting increasingly ugly. "Get behind me!" Zeal hissed to Resus and Cleo.

Rooney chuckled nastily as he and the crowd of convicts closed in. "It seems like just about everyone here is delighted to see you and your little friends. . . ."

Chillchase began to back away. "It's me you want. Let the children go."

Higgs licked his thick, scaly lips. "And mith the chanthe of a tasthty meal?"

"Save a leg for me," gurgled another voice. "I like a bit of vampire." A zombie appeared from

23

the other direction, leading a second pack of furious offenders.

"We're surrounded," gulped Resus.

"Any ideas?" asked Cleo nervously.

"There!" cried Chillchase, pointing to a unicorn tied to a post outside one of the huts. "If I can distract them, you two get out of here on that!"

"Do we have to?" Cleo gulped. "The last time I tried to ride one of those, it skewered me with its horn."

"Hang around here and you'll be skewered by a hungry lizard instead," Resus pointed out. "Over a roasting fire! So no complaints—we're taking the unicorn."

"What will you do?" Cleo asked Zeal.

"I'll be fine," replied the Tracker. "I'll meet you at the tree where I found Resus. Now, we just need some sort of distraction . . ."

Right on cue, one side of the hospital hut suddenly exploded in a shower of wood and tin, and Luke's werewolf sprang out. It leaped through the crowd, using its powerful paws to swipe Rooney and Higgs out of the way, then stood, fangs dripping, as if awaiting further instructions.

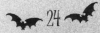

24

"I thought you said he was injured!" exclaimed Resus.

"He *was!*" Cleo insisted.

"Thank goodness he has more control over his transformations than he did last time we were here," said Resus.

"The tables have turned," Chillchase declared, taking a step forward and scratching Luke's werewolf behind the ear. "Move aside and let us go."

The leprechaun laughed scornfully. "Most of us here want your skin, Chillchase! Your doggy can't take us all down."

The Tracker calmly pulled his sunglasses from his pocket and slipped them back on. "He doesn't need to take them all down, Rooney," he said. "Just *you.*"

The leprechaun glanced nervously up at the snarling werewolf, then back at Chillchase. "Let them through!" he commanded the baying crowd.

"But I haven't tathted meat in nearly theven yearth," moaned Higgs.

"I don't care!" snapped Rooney. "I said, let them through!"

Reluctantly, the angry group parted. Zeal Chillchase strode through the crowd, Luke's wolf

25

beside him, teeth bared. Resus and Cleo followed closely.

"I'll get you!" Rooney spat. "You might get away this time, but I'll find you!"

Chillchase climbed onto the unicorn's back after Resus and Cleo and glared down at the seething leprechaun. "I look forward to it," he growled.

Then, with a click of his heels, the Tracker sent the unicorn crashing through the frail wooden gate and off across the dreary plains of the Underlands, Luke's werewolf racing along behind.

Chapter Four
The Plan

When the group reached Zeal Chillchase's
campsite, the Tracker helped Resus and Cleo
down from the unicorn before sending it running
free across the plains. Luke's werewolf slumped
to the ground and began to transform back into
human form.

Cleo dashed over to him. At first she couldn't
see the wound on his leg through the thick brown

fur, but as that began to recede, the neatly stitched scar slowly became visible. "You need to rest," she told Luke.

"I feel fine," he retorted.

"Luke Watson, you stay right there and don't move until I tell you!"

Her friend smiled. "Whatever you say!"

Resus unclipped his vampire cape and lay it over Luke. "Best idea," he whispered. "Don't argue with her."

Chillchase sat beneath the blackened tree and began to stuff his few belongings into a battered old backpack. "We need to open a Hex Hatch and leave as soon as possible," he said.

"Do you think Rooney and his gang will come looking for us?" asked Resus.

"It's possible," replied the Tracker.

"Are we going right back to Scream Street?" asked Cleo.

Zeal Chillchase shook his head. "We're going to China first."

"*China?*" exclaimed Resus.

"A former G.H.O.U.L. Tracker I know lives there," Chillchase explained. "She'll be able to help restore my power and provide us with supplies."

Cleo looked at him. "What supplies?"

Zeal Chillchase reached up to snap a dead twig from the tree and use it to scrawl some numbers in the black earth. "The way I see it, we have six tasks ahead of us. One: Return to Scream Street. Two: Retrieve *The G.H.O.U.L. Guide*. Three: Evict all the normals from Scream Street. Four: Resurrect Samuel Skipstone from the pages of *The G.H.O.U.L. Guide*. Five: Get Skipstone to transform into his werewolf. Six: Return the final relic—the werewolf's claw—to Skipstone, and in doing so close the doorway forever."

"Six tasks," murmured Luke. "Just like the six relics."

"Exactly," said Chillchase. "And if we want to succeed, we'll need supplies."

"I've got loads of stuff inside my cape," Resus reminded him. "Surely there's no need to go all the way to China."

"I suspect that what we need can't be found inside any vampire cape," said Zeal. "Black-market Hex Hatch spells for a start, plus

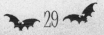

reanimation gel to bring Skipstone back—and we'll need the shell of a dragon's egg, too."

"What for?" asked Luke sitting up, the cape still wrapped around his shoulders.

"You'll need a strong sleeping potion to use on the werewolf," Chillchase explained. "An angry werewolf won't sit still while you reattach its claw. The shell of a dragon's egg will give you the strongest kind of sleeping potion possible."

"That's right!" exclaimed Resus. "That's what Cuffy said when we were trying to catch that baby yeti."

"Where can we get a dragon's eggshell?" asked Luke.

"Don't tell me," said Cleo. "China!"

Chillchase nodded. "My contact should be able to provide us with one."

"And you're sure she won't tell G.H.O.U.L. what we're up to?" asked Resus.

"I'm certain," said Chillchase. "She resigned as a Tracker shortly after Acrid Belcher took charge and started ordering everyone around."

"I'd forgotten about Belcher," said Luke. "What should we do about him?"

"You leave Acrid Belcher to me," answered Chillchase. "First things first . . ."

"Right," said Resus, jumping up. "China it is!"

"But Luke has to rest," Cleo argued.

"I'm fine, really," said Luke, climbing to his feet and handing the cape back to Resus. "A bit tired, but my leg's healing nicely."

"All right," grumbled Cleo. "Then Mr. Chillchase might as well give us our gutweed."

"Our what?" asked Luke.

"Eating gutweed turns you into a shapeshifter," Cleo explained. "Temporarily, anyway. We can use it to disguise ourselves once we're back on Scream Street."

Resus pulled a frond of gutweed from his pocket and stuffed it into his mouth. "It tastes vile," he said, "but you can do stuff like this!" He shut his eyes, and within seconds his skin and muscles had faded away to reveal the bones underneath.

"That's incredible!" said Luke.

"I know." The skeletal Resus grinned. "Give it a try!"

Zeal handed Luke some gutweed, and

tentatively he put it in his mouth and began to chew. The taste was awful—like every bowl of brussels sprouts his mom had ever served on Christmas Day strained through a pair of sweaty socks. Before long, however, he could feel his muscles begin to tingle.

"Now close your eyes and think of someone else," Chillchase commanded. "Maybe someone you know from Scream Street."

Gradually, Luke's skin began to peel and turn green. Weeping sores and boils appeared on his cheeks, and his eyes grew dull. His clothes became rags and his fingers twisted out of shape.

Cleo squealed with excitement. "You look like Doug!"

Luke opened his eyes and peered down at his new zombie form. "Cool, dude!"

"My turn," said the mummy, taking a piece of gutweed for herself. "But I don't know what you're moaning about—this tastes like my dad's nettle turnovers."

"Told you it was disgusting," said Resus.

Curly blond hair began to sprout from the bandages on Cleo's scalp. Her eyes grew bigger and twinkled in the weak sunlight, and soon she was swathed in a shimmering, silver silk dress.

Luke stared. "You're . . . You're a witch!" he said with a gasp.

"Complete with enchantment charm," added Resus.

Zeal Chillchase gave the remaining gutweed to Resus to look after. "It's time to turn back," he instructed. "Just think of something from your own lives, like a member of your family or something you keep at home."

Within seconds the trio looked like their normal selves again. "I was just getting used to that," said Cleo, grinning.

Luke surveyed the desolate landscape around them. "I don't think I'll ever get used to anything in this place," he said with a shiver. "Let's get out of here."

The Tracker began to move his hands through the air, muttering the spell that would allow him to open the Hex Hatch. The strain of using the very last of his power was clear, and soon Zeal was breathing heavily and sweating.

Eventually, the portal was ready. On the

other side, the group could see a bustling Chinese market, stalls piled high with all kinds of unfamiliar merchandise.

"Last one in buys the noodles!" cried Resus, and he jumped through.

"Won't be me," said Cleo, following. She turned back and held her hand out to Luke. "Here, let me help—"

"I'm fine," Luke insisted, and he limped through after her.

Then, just as Zeal Chillchase was swinging the backpack over his shoulder and preparing to follow, a large lizard dropped out of the sky beside him, a small red-haired man in a green suit clinging to its back.

"Did you forget lamias could fly, Chillchase?" asked Rooney, jumping to the ground. "All we had to do was climb high enough to spot you— and there you were!"

Chillchase raced for the Hex Hatch, but Rooney caught hold of his long, leather coat, dragging him back.

"Zeal!" yelled Luke, trying to grab the Tracker's hand, but the unstable Hex Hatch was beginning to fail.

"Say good-bye to your friends, dead man!" screeched the leprechaun with delight. Then, with alarming finality, the Hex Hatch snapped shut.

"NO!" Luke shouted, waving his hands in the air in a vain attempt to reopen the window, but it was too late.

Zeal Chillchase was stuck in the Underlands.

Luke slumped against a stall selling
herbs and spices. "It's my fault," he moaned. All
around them, shoppers bustled through the busy
marketplace in the warm sunshine.

"There's nothing you could have done," said
Cleo.

"We didn't know Rooney would find us so
quickly," Resus added.

"Yes, but if Zeal hadn't waited for me to rest before he opened the Hex Hatch, we'd have been here long before that stupid leprechaun could find us!"

As he spoke, a young Chinese woman with a faint eerie glow around her set up an easel in front of the trio. "You want portrait?" she asked in heavily accented English.

"No, thank you," said Luke as politely as he could, and they moved away.

"There's no point worrying about who's to blame," said Cleo. "We need to keep going. It's what Zeal would tell us to do if he were here."

"But how?" asked Resus. "I might not pay much attention at school, but even I know that there are more than a billion people in China. How are we supposed to find the person Zeal Chillchase was planning to meet?"

The artist picked up her easel and scurried along to stand in front of the children again. "Portrait very good!"

"I'm sure they are," said Cleo kindly, "but we're not really in the mood right now." She led the boys over to a stall selling clay pots and began to examine one without any real interest. "Zeal

must have opened the Hex Hatch here for a reason," she said. "His contact must be here in this town—wherever 'here' is."

"OK," said Resus. "So that narrows it down to several thousand. It could still take us weeks—and we can't exactly stop people in the street and ask them if they used to be a Tracker for G.H.O.U.L.!"

The artist scuttled through the crowds to catch up with them once again. "Portrait time!"

Trying to hide his irritation, Resus took a deep breath. "We don't have any money."

"Portrait free!" the artist said, beaming.

Resus shook his head and turned away. Luke and Cleo followed him to a table piled high with unfamiliar fruit.

"If this person has been a Tracker for G.H.O.U.L., she must be one of us," said Luke. "A vampire, or a zombie, or a shapeshifter, or something. We just need to figure out how to spot her."

"Without G.H.O.U.L. spotting us first," Resus added. "If we attract attention, we'll be back in the Underlands faster than a pickpocketing poltergeist!"

"Speaking of attracting attention. . . ." began

Luke. The young artist was just behind them again, her paintbrush darting across the canvas. "Look, I'm really sorry," he said, "but we don't want to have our picture painted!"

"Portrait done." The artist smiled, and spun the easel around to show them. The picture showed the trio deep in conversation in the middle of the bustling market.

"It's very nice," said Resus, "but . . ." He stopped and stared. In the drawing, Luke was sporting a werewolf's tail.

"If you really don't want to attract attention, I suggest you stay quiet and follow me," hissed the artist, this time in perfect English.

Stunned, the trio followed her to a quiet corner of the market. "Are you Zeal Chillchase's friend?" Luke asked tentatively. Close up, he could see that the girl's strangely glowing skin was also bumpy and rough, like alligator hide.

The girl nodded. "I'm Icus—and you three stepped through a Hex Hatch in full view of the public. Zeal must be in real trouble to pull a stunt like that. This isn't a G.H.O.U.L. community, and people like us have to keep a low profile or we'll end up in one. Where *is* Chillchase, by the way?"

"He didn't make it," said Luke.

Icus listened carefully as Luke, Resus, and Cleo explained how they came to be there, why they had collected the founding fathers' relics, and, as they neared the end of their quest to close the doorway, how they had been arrested by Acrid Belcher and banished to the Underlands.

"Belcher!" muttered Icus angrily. "He's the reason I left G.H.O.U.L. He treats normals the same way as this Sir Otto guy clearly treats people like us." She took a deep breath to calm her temper. "What can I do to help?"

"We need a Hex Hatch spell to get us back home," said Resus. "And some reanimation gel to help bring back an old friend."

"We also need to make a sleeping potion strong enough to subdue a werewolf," added Luke. "Apparently, for that we'll need a piece of shell from a dragon's egg."

"A dragon's egg?" Icus smiled. "I know just the person. . . ."

Half an hour later, Luke, Resus, and Cleo found themselves waiting nervously in a dark alley behind a restaurant. As soon as they had arrived,

Icus had wished them luck and left. "I wouldn't put it past Belcher to be watching former Trackers like me," she had explained. "I don't want to put you in any extra danger."

"Well," said Resus, prodding at the remainder of what appeared to be a piece of chicken with his shoe. "This is a lovely place for a meeting. What did Icus say the guy's name was?"

"She didn't," replied Luke. "She just said we'd know him when we saw him."

"That's a bit vague," Cleo commented.

"And that's the way I like it," said a voice from the shadows.

"I like it better than you," said another.

Whatever the trio was expecting to step into the glow of the streetlight, it wasn't this. The creature was dressed in a bright orange suit and matching shoes. Two heads sprouted from a single body—although each face only had one eye.

"A cyclops!" exclaimed Resus.

"*He's* a cyclops," corrected the first head, nodding toward the other. "I think you'll find that *I'm* perfectly normal."

"Oh, don't listen to him," said the second head. "And we're actually a *biclops*."

"A what?" asked Cleo.

"A biclops," replied the second head. "A cyclops with two heads and two eyes—therefore, a biclops! My name is Stan, and this ugly mug here is Ollie."

"Ooh, watch who you're calling ugly," snapped Ollie. "We're twins, remember?"

"Twins, my nostrils!" cried Stan. "I'm better looking than you'll ever be."

"Excuse me," interrupted Luke. "But Icus said you might be able to get us a Hex Hatch spell and a dragon's egg."

"*I* can," said Stan smugly. "The only thing *he'll* get you is trouble."

"How dare you?" retorted Ollie. "I know exactly where all our spells are stored. Probably because *I'm* the only one who ever cleans the storeroom!"

"You never do!" cried Stan. "I swept up all that broken glass last week."

"Well, who broke the glass, hmm?" teased Ollie. "You're the one who knocked over the bottle of wine because you can't see properly out of your ONE EYE!"

"That's not fair," sobbed Stan. "I was born like this—and so were you."

"Yes, but I've learned to cope with my visual limitations. You're too busy preening to give it a second thought!"

At that, Stan raised the hand on his side and slapped Ollie across the cheek. Ollie looked shocked for a moment, then returned the slap

with the other hand. Within seconds, the biclops was rolling around on the ground, fighting with itself.

"Stop it!" shouted Luke, grabbing the hand on Ollie's side while Resus grabbed the other. "This is ridiculous!"

The biclops climbed to its feet, smoothing the creases out of its suit. "*He* started it," mumbled Stan sulkily.

"I did not!" cried Ollie. "You were the one who said—"

"That's enough!" exclaimed Luke. "Now, can you give us the things we need, or shall we take our business elsewhere?"

"We've got what you need," Ollie assured him.

"But it depends on what you've got to trade," added Stan.

Luke turned to Resus. "Over to you. . . ."

The vampire began to rummage around inside his cape. "I've got a pair of hedge trimmers, a table-tennis bat, a sombrero—"

"I'd look good in that!" cried Stan, snatching the hat from Resus.

"You haven't got anything to wear with it," declared Ollie.

"It'll look wonderful with anything," Stan retorted.

"There's a baby's rattle," continued Resus, "two lightbulbs . . . a scarf . . ."

"Now you're talking," said Ollie, taking the blue-and-white woolen scarf and wrapping it around his neck. "What else?"

Resus continued to produce random items from his cape while the biclops gave a running commentary. "A silver-plated picture frame . . ."

"Tacky!"

"A jar of pickles . . ."

"Does he *want* our breath to smell?"

"Yours already smells."

"Oh, be quiet!"

"A rugby ball, a train conductor's whistle, a pair of sunglasses . . ."

"STOP!" cried both Stan and Ollie at once.

Resus paused. "What? You want the sunglasses?"

Ollie snatched them from Resus, and pressing its heads together, the biclops just about managed to squeeze the dark glasses over its two faces.

"We look wonderful," said Stan with a sigh.

"Like a dream," cooed Ollie.

45

"Thank you," they both said together.

"You're welcome," said Luke. "But don't forget your side of the bargain."

"Of course!" Stan beamed. He plunged his hand into the pocket on his side of the suit jacket and produced a jar of clear goo, which he handed to Luke.

"This must be the reanimation gel," Luke said.

Ollie gave Cleo two sheets of paper. "This one looks like the Hex Hatch spell," said Resus, taking one of them. "But where's the eggshell?"

"You said—" Luke looked up, but the biclops had disappeared. He, Luke, and Cleo were alone in the alley.

"They conned us out of the egg!" Resus cried.

"No, they didn't," said Cleo, examining the second sheet of paper. On it was drawn a map that showed a cave marked DRAGON'S LAIR. "I think we have to get it ourselves!"

Chapter Six
The Bridge

Luke clenched his teeth as the wheels of the rickshaw crashed into yet another pothole. If he wasn't careful, he would bite off the end of his tongue before they got anywhere near the dragon's cave.

The trio had had to barter even more items from Resus's cloak in return for the trip. The driver—a local man—was racing up ahead, pulling the children along at breakneck speed in what was little more than a wooden wheelbarrow.

"Do you think we're nearly there?" asked Cleo, clinging on as the driver turned a corner, one of the rickshaw's wheels lifting clear off the ground. It spun wildly in the air for a few seconds, then crashed back down onto the road with a thump.

Luke struggled to hold the biclops's map steady enough to read. "We've definitely left the center of the town," he said. "And as far as I can tell, we're traveling north."

Resus glanced up at the buildings around them. The shops and food stands had long since given way to small houses and blocks of apartments. Ahead, he could see where the buildings stopped altogether, opening up to green fields that stretched toward the horizon. "Let's just hope he's taking us in the right direction," he muttered.

After another twenty minutes or so, the rickshaw driver came to a sudden stop at a battered fence. He turned to the trio and began to point at the fields around them, shaking his head. "No go!" he barked. "No go!"

Luke climbed out. "What do you mean?" he asked.

"Stop now," continued the driver. "No go!"

"I think he's saying he won't take us any far-ther," said Cleo helpfully.

"But we've paid him to take us all the way to the dragon's lair," said Luke. "At least I *think* we have. . . ." He turned to Resus. "What did you give him?"

"A set of coloring pens, a tube of toothpaste, and a pair of inflatable armbands."

Luke turned back to the driver. "We'll give you more if you take us farther." Resus pulled a teddy bear from his cape and waved it as allur-ingly as he could.

The rickshaw driver shook his head again. "No go!" he insisted, then he ushered Cleo and Resus out of the seat, spun the vehicle around, and began to race back the way they had come.

Cleo took the teddy from Resus and gave it a quick cuddle. "I guess we're walking from here, then," she said.

A while later, Luke, Resus, and Cleo found them-selves trudging through fields of long grass. The town was nothing more than a thin, gray line on the horizon behind them, and ahead lay the foot-hills of a desolate mountain range.

 49

"Does this strike either of you as odd?" Luke asked.

"What, that we've been abandoned in the middle of nowhere and ended up walking for miles toward certain danger?" questioned Resus. "Nope, not in the slightest!"

Luke grinned. "That does sound like us—but I meant these fields."

"I've never seen grass this long before," Cleo put in.

"Exactly," said Luke. "But you'd think all this land would be used for something."

"Like what?" asked Resus.

"I dunno," replied Luke with a shrug. "Growing food or something."

"Well, for your information, this is the fallow field in a yearly cycle of crop rotation. Leaving the grass to grow improves soil structure and helps replenish nitrogen."

Luke stopped walking and stared at Cleo. "Excuse me?"

"I didn't say anything!" replied the mummy. "Resus . . . ?"

"Since when did I know anything about crop rotation?" asked the vampire.

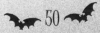

"You don't need to—I'm an expert on the subject!"

Intrigued, the trio followed the voice. Luke parted the long grass with his hands and saw a pair of eyes staring back at him. He cleared a bit more to reveal an extremely small woman standing before them, hands on hips. "Although, I admit, the crop rotation cycle is not the only reason why this field is untouched by either crops or livestock."

"It, er . . . isn't?" asked Luke.

"Nope," replied the tiny figure. "That'll be 'cause everyone's terrified of the dragon."

"Dragon?" cried Resus. "So we *are* heading in the right direction!"

"You're on the right path for the dragon," agreed the figure. "Seen it with my own eyes."

"Who *are* you?" Cleo asked, peering down into the grass.

"Meg G. Nome, at your service!" The little woman beamed. "Wearer of the Boots of Magic and Keeper of the Rock of Wonder."

"The Boots of *what*?" asked Resus.

"Magic," said Meg, grinning. She lifted her leg to show off a shiny blue boot. "That's them there—well, one of them, anyway!"

Resus frowned. "So . . . what exactly is magic about them?"

"They let me walk anywhere I want to go," explained the gnome.

"That's it?"

Meg shrugged. "What else would you expect a pair of boots to do?"

"And the Rock of Wonder?" asked Cleo.

The gnome frowned. "That doesn't walk anywhere. It's a rock."

"No, I mean—what *is* the Rock of Wonder?"

"Ah . . ." replied Meg as mysteriously as she could. "The Rock of Wonder is a rock . . . of wonder!"

"You're messing with us," grunted Resus.

"I am not!" insisted Meg.

"Save your breath," said the vampire. "I don't want to see the Rock of Wonder, or sit on the Chair of Destiny, or even use the Toothbrush of Secrets. . . ."

A look of terror flashed across the gnome's tiny face. "Who told you about the Toothbrush of Secrets?" she asked.

Resus sighed. "For goodness' sake—"

 52

"STOP!" commanded Meg. "Or you'll fall into the Chasm of Doom!"

"The *what?*" scoffed Resus.

"The Chasm of Doom," Meg repeated. "It's filled with the Ghosts of Regret and the Monsters of Oblivion."

"Keep talking and you'll get a kick on the bum from the Foot of Irritation," said Resus, beginning to walk on. "We need to find the— *Aargh!*"

Luke leaped forward and grabbed his friend just in time. The pair was standing on the edge of a ravine. Swirls of thick mist obscured the bottom, so there was no knowing how deep it was.

"That'll be the Chasm of Doom, then," said Cleo.

"That's the one," confirmed Meg. "And over there on the other side are the Mountains of Terror and the Cave of Certain Death."

"Don't tell me . . ." said Luke. "The Cave of Certain Death is where we'll find the dragon."

"Exactly!"

"How do we get across the Chasm of Doom?" Cleo asked cautiously.

"Easy," said the gnome. "You use the Bridge

53

of Truth. I shall activate the Boots of Magic to show you where it is." With that, she strode off along the edge of the chasm, head held high.

"We'd better follow her," said Luke, although that was easier said than done. The gnome moved quickly, and it was difficult to spot her in the long grass. Eventually, however, the four of them came to a long rope bridge that spanned the canyon.

"Behold the Bridge of Truth!" announced Meg.

"It's very nice," said Cleo kindly. "Thanks for all your help." She was about to step onto the bridge when the gnome grabbed her hand and pulled her back.

"You can't just walk across the Bridge of Truth!" she squealed.

"You can't?" said Cleo.

"Of course not!" cried Meg. "It's not called the Bridge of Truth for nothing. You have to tell the bridge-keeper—that's me—a truth before you can proceed."

"So you want to hear us say something true before we can cross?" said Resus.

"Now you're getting it." The gnome grinned. She took Luke by the hand and pulled him toward the bridge. "Tell me about your first love."

"Well, there hasn't really been . . ." mumbled Luke, his cheeks flushing red. "I mean, there was a girl at my old school who I really liked, but I didn't tell anyone. . . ."

"You may cross." Meg smiled.

"Oh, er . . . right. Thanks." Luke stepped out onto the bridge and began cautiously to make his way across the thin wooden planks that were strung between two lengths of rough, twisted rope that spanned the ravine. A second pair of ropes hung at waist height, and Luke gripped these tightly as he made his way across, trying not to look down.

"You next!" said the gnome, turning to Resus. "What is your greatest fear?"

"That's easy enough," replied Resus with a sigh. "It's that my family wouldn't want me anymore because I'm not a real vampire."

"You may cross."

With a glance at Cleo, Resus followed Luke onto the rope bridge.

"Lastly, you." Meg took Cleo's hand. "Tell me what you've done that you are most ashamed of."

Cleo's eyes widened. "I don't think I want to," she said. "Can you ask me something else?"

The gnome shook her head. "Once the Question of Interest has been asked, it cannot be unasked. Now, what are you most ashamed of doing?"

Cleo gulped. "I . . . I once chased an explorer out of my tomb back in Egypt."

 56

"There," said Meg, "that wasn't so bad, was it? Now you can cross."

"Thank you," croaked Cleo, and she stepped out onto the first plank.

Suddenly, the bridge began to jerk violently from side to side, and the trio had to cling on for dear life. The planks bucked beneath their feet, threatening to hurl them into the seemingly bottomless chasm below.

"What's happening?" yelled Luke.

Meg fixed the trio with a stern look. "One of you has not told the truth!" she declared.

Chapter Seven
The Lair

Luke's foot slipped between two of the planks, and he fell face-first onto the narrow walkway of the bridge as it continued to rock and sway like a rodeo bull.

"What did you *say*?" he bellowed to Resus, his palms burning as the rope tried to pull free of his grasp.

"It wasn't me!" Resus retorted. "You *know* my greatest fear is being cast out for not being a real vampire. It must have been you."

"But I told the truth!" Luke yelled back. "I had a crush on Nicola Shepherd at my old school. It can't have—*Oof!*" The rest of his sentence was lost as one of the planks jolted upward and smacked him in the chin.

Resus struggled to look back over his shoulder. "But that means . . ."

"I didn't want that question!" screeched Cleo as she was flung around like a rag doll. "I didn't want to say what I'm most ashamed of!"

"You *have* to!" shouted Resus. "Or we'll all end up at the bottom of the Chasm of Doom as flat as the Pancakes of Kersplat!"

Cleo looked pleadingly at Meg, who watched calmly from the bank as though this kind of thing happened every day. "Please make it stop!" she begged.

"I can't," the gnome called back. "The Bridge of Truth has a mind of its own—and it doesn't like being lied to. There's only one way to stop it."

Suddenly, one end of the bridge rose up like a tidal wave, and Cleo was flipped right over

the side. She managed to keep one hand on the handrail, but her legs were now dangling free over the churning mist below.

"Cleo!" cried Luke. "You have to tell the truth—NOW!"

Closing her eyes tightly, Cleo roared, "I stole a necklace from the emporium!"

As quickly as it had started, the bridge stopped moving, leaving the trio swaying gently in the breeze. Resus and Luke raced back to pull Cleo to safety, and the three of them sank down, trying to catch their breath.

"You stole a necklace?" Luke asked Cleo.

Wiping away tears, Cleo reached into her bandages and produced a silver chain with a sparkling sapphire flower pendant hanging from it. "I'm sorry," she sobbed.

"I've never seen Eefa selling anything like that," said Resus.

"It wasn't strictly from Everwell's Emporium," Cleo admitted. "It was from *Higginbotham's* Emporium, in nineteen seventy-one—when we chased the baby yeti through your cloak. I'd never seen anything so beautiful, and I just couldn't help myself."

 60

"That doesn't sound like the sort of thing you'd do," Luke said, surprised.

"I know," said Cleo. "I kept telling myself not to, but it felt as if the necklace was calling to me. So as soon as Cuffy wasn't looking . . ." She sniffed. "I'm sorry."

"It's OK," Luke assured her. "We're all safe now." He peered back toward the edge of the ravine. "I see that Meg has disappeared."

"Probably gone home to make herself a Pie of Tastiness," quipped Resus.

Cleo gave a weak smile. "Can we get off this bridge now?" she asked.

"Good idea," said Luke, helping her to her feet. "We don't want to keep the terrifying dragon waiting, after all."

Resus followed them onto the far bank. "Thanks for the reminder," he said. "For a minute there, I was almost starting to enjoy myself!"

"Are we really going to do this?" whispered Resus as he, Luke, and Cleo crept into a cave set in the side of the mountain. "Are we really going to try to get a piece of shell from a dragon's egg?"

Luke nodded. "Without the dragon finding out and burning us to a cinder, that is."

Resus grinned. "There's nothing like a challenge. . . ."

"Can you two hear something?" asked Cleo.

The boys strained their ears. "I can't," the vampire admitted. "Just the breeze blowing in from outside."

"Except the breeze *isn't* blowing in from outside," said Cleo. "It's going in the opposite direction—and it's blowing in a regular pattern. Like breathing."

"She's right!" exclaimed Luke after a moment. "It *is* breathing!" The trio kept walking, the space around them widening until they arrived at a vast cavern, lit by weak beams of sunlight seeping in from some unseen entrance far above.

"This is incredible," said Resus. "All we need now is—"

The words caught in his throat as his cape flapped out behind him and he realized that, just ahead, lay a huge, sleeping dragon.

The creature was at least the size of a house, and covered in glistening silvery-blue scales. It lay curled up in a giant nest made from branches and bundles of crisp, yellow grass, and as its snout was facing the children, they were hit by a powerful gust of wind each time the dragon breathed out.

"That," whispered Luke, "is awesome."

"And dangerous," Cleo reminded him. "Let's get a bit of shell and go."

"That might not be so easy," Resus commented. "I can't see any eggs."

"He's right," Luke said. "What if the dragon hasn't got any?"

"She's laid some eggs all right," Cleo assured them.

"How do you know it's a she?" asked Resus.

Cleo rolled her eyes. "Female dragons have longer snouts than males. And that"—she pointed to the creature's head—"is an elongated snout. Plus, they only make nests when they're ready to lay eggs—and I'd say that one was made quite a while ago."

"How on earth do you know all this stuff?" asked Luke.

"Simple," replied Cleo. "I paid attention

when Dr. Skully taught us about it. As I seem to remember, you two spent the entire lesson drawing zombie hedgehogs in your notebooks."

Resus glanced around the cavern. "So . . . where are these eggs?"

Cleo let out a grunt of frustration. "In the nest, of course. Under the dragon."

"This is going to be even harder than I thought," said Luke.

"Don't be so negative," said Cleo. "We only need a bit of shell, and we should be able to scrape that from the outside of one of the eggs without harming it. In fact, we might even get lucky and find a few broken bits in the bottom of the nest."

Resus looked at the branches, crushed under the weight of the dragon's bulk. "So we have to go over to the nest and search?"

"Well, she's not going to bring the eggs to us, is she?" said Cleo, and before Resus could reply, she was darting across the cavern toward the sleeping beast.

"Cleo, wait!" hissed Luke, but it was too late. The mummy was already trying to lift the dragon's massive tail and peer into the nest beneath.

By the time the boys had caught up with her,

Cleo had squeezed her head between the dragon's body and the twisted branches. After a moment, she reappeared.

"No bits of broken shell, I'm afraid," she said. "And the eggs are far too big to lift out. There's only one way we can do this."

"How?" asked Luke.

"One of us will have to climb into the nest."

Chapter Eight

The Nest

Resus and Cleo grabbed the sleeping dragon's tail and lifted it as high as they could, allowing Luke to squeeze into the darkness of the nest below, a flashlight clamped between his teeth.

Once his friends had lowered the tail again, Luke found himself pressed into the sticks and dead grass beneath him. The thin beam of the flashlight had little effect in the gloom, and the heat was stifling.

Grabbing a couple of branches, Luke was able to wriggle forward, the flashlight's beam glimmering weakly off the dragon's underbelly. He was beginning to sweat, but he continued to climb deeper and deeper into the nest until he reached the three large eggs in the center.

Twisting himself around into a sitting position, Luke pulled out the penknife and Horror Heights–themed lunchbox Resus had given him, then reached for the nearest egg. He began to scrape at the shell with the knife, holding the lunchbox underneath to catch the tiny fragments. He didn't know how much eggshell was required to make the sleeping potion, so he planned to fill the box and hope that was enough.

A fine, bluish dust came away with each scrape and seemed to hang thickly in the air. Luke wiped the sweat from his eyes and shifted the knife round to tackle another part of the egg. The lunchbox was about a third full now, and if he continued at this rate he would—

Suddenly the egg jolted as the baby inside moved, and Luke was thrown backward. The penknife was knocked out of his hand and the contents of the lunchbox spilled over his lap. Now he'd have to start all over again!

As Luke felt around for the lost knife, he heard a rumbling and the nest began to creak. The dragon was moving! Luke was shaken from side to side, the flashlight still gripped between his teeth, its beam swinging to and fro like a wartime searchlight. It was then that he spotted the knife — embedded between two glimmering scales at the base of the dragon's tail.

From the back of the cave, Resus and Cleo looked on in horror as the dragon rose up and roared. The sound was unlike anything Resus had ever heard, and he quickly covered his ears. Then the creature's tail swung across the cavern. The vampire hurled himself to the ground to avoid being hit.

The dragon stomped across the shaking stone floor, still shrieking.

Cleo landed with a crash beside Resus, and the two of them watched as Luke, coated in fine

blue powder, appeared groggily from the bowels of the nest.

"What did he do to make her so angry?" hissed the mummy.

Resus pushed Cleo's head down as the tail swept over them again. "That!" he exclaimed, pointing to the knife as it flashed by, still embedded in the creature's hide. "He's only gone and stabbed the dragon in the bum."

"I didn't mean to!" protested Luke. "The egg jumped and pushed me backward!"

At the sound of Luke's voice, the dragon swung its head around and roared again—and this time its cry was accompanied by a jet of red-hot flame.

"Luke!" bellowed Resus. "You have to get out of there!"

Luke's head reappeared above the rim of the nest, but Cleo gestured frantically for him to stay down. "No, don't move!" she yelled. "The dragon won't risk harming her eggs. As long as you stay where you are, you're safe!"

The dragon spun around to face the pair and let loose another sheet of searing flame. Resus

pulled Cleo down again, feeling his eyebrows being singed by the blast. "But *we're* not safe now, are we, blabbermouth? We need to open the Hex Hatch and get out of here!"

"What about the egg?" said Cleo.

"I guess we'll have to take one with us. . . ."

Suddenly, a large shadow fell across Resus and Cleo, and the dragon's head loomed over the pile of rocks where they were hiding, its snout sniffing at the air just above them.

"JUMP!" cried Resus, and the pair managed to dive aside just as a jet of flame hit the spot where they had been crouching. They raced for the nest and dived inside, tumbling down through the branches and dead grass to land beside the eggs.

"Are you OK?" Luke asked, crawling over to join them. "I heard the dragon roar and I thought—"

"We're fine," said Resus. "And—even better—I've got an *eggs*-ellent plan!"

"I hope you're not *yolking*," Luke quipped back. Resus grinned and gave him a high five.

"We don't have time for this!" Cleo snapped.

"OK," said Resus. "Here's what we'll do.

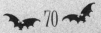

Luke will activate the Hex Hatch spell over on the far side of the cave while I grab one of the eggs."

"I don't think we should steal an egg," warned Cleo. "It'll make the dragon angry."

"Yeah," said Luke, "'cause it's been the model of calm up until now!"

"We're not *stealing* the egg," Resus explained, "we're borrowing it. Once we've scraped off enough of the shell, we'll get Eefa or Twinkle to open another Hex Hatch so we can return it."

"OK," Cleo conceded, "but we have to bring it back."

"Once the Hex Hatch is open," Resus continued, "Cleo will distract the dragon so I can grab an egg, then we'll all make a break for home."

"One question," said Luke. "How do I get over to the far side of the cave with that thing out there?"

He had barely finished speaking when the dragon's head plunged into the nest, mouth open and teeth bared. Giant jaws snapped together, gripping Luke's T-shirt and lifting him into the air. With a flick of its powerful neck, the creature flung him across the cavern, where he landed with a sickening crash.

"Well," said Resus. "That seems to have done the trick!" He clambered up the side of the nest and saw that the dragon was now making its way across the cave toward Luke. "Cleo!" he hissed. "You have to go NOW!"

The mummy scrambled up beside him. "What am I supposed to do?"

"Do what you do best," Resus replied. "Go out there and cause trouble!"

Chapter Nine
The Zombies

Luke shook his head

to clear it. His back ached
where he had crashed into the wall of the cave,
and he could already feel bruises forming under his
torn T-shirt. His vision was blurred, but he could
just make out something large and blue heading
his way. No, not just see it—he could feel it. The
ground was shaking beneath him.

The dragon thundered toward him

and Luke knew he had to move. He tried to stand, but a bolt of pain shot through his head. The dragon would be on him any second, and this time—

"Hey, big girl!" yelled Cleo, jumping down in front of the furious beast. "Why don't you pick on someone your own size?"

"What are you doing?" Luke cried in amazement.

"Saving your life!" shouted the mummy. "Now hurry up and read out that Hex Hatch spell!" She spun back around to face the dragon. "I mean it, ugly mug—I'm the one you want!" She snatched up a rock and threw it at the enraged creature.

The dragon twisted around and gave chase, breathing out another plume of searing flame. Cleo dropped under the jet of fire and rolled quickly to one side.

Luke pulled the paper from his pocket. The words, written in a shaky hand and already difficult to read, swam across the page in front of him. He held the spell at arm's length and willed himself to focus. The lives of his friends depended on it.

Inside the nest, Resus grabbed the nearest egg and tried to lift it. It was far heavier than he had imagined: helping his parents move their new wardrobe up the stairs at home had been easier, and that was made of Transylvanian oak.

A cry echoed around the cave: "You call that breathing fire? My dad has fiercer breath after a bowl of nettle chili!"

Resus grinned. Cleo was still keeping the dragon distracted—and appeared to be enjoying herself! He strained to lift the egg again and prayed that Luke was close to opening the Hex Hatch.

"*Macker dah . . . smolian . . .*" Luke struggled to read the words of the spell. His vision was clearing fast, but the language of magic was completely alien to him. For all he knew, this wasn't a Hex Hatch spell at all and he was about to transform himself into a vase of man-eating roses. "*Vass trashler deese . . . tarda!*"

Suddenly, a tiny hole appeared in the air before him. Through it he could see what looked like the living room of a house. He couldn't be certain it was a house on Scream Street, but frankly, anywhere was better than here right

now. Tossing the parchment aside, he pushed his fingers into the hole and began to stretch it wider, as he had seen Zeal Chillchase do.

Cleo ducked into a recess in the rock as another blast of flame shot past her—this one closer than before—and it was a second or two before she realized that the bandages around her feet had caught alight. *Resus would probably tell me to hotfoot it out of here,* she thought with a smile as she batted out the flames.

The dragon's head swung back into view, blocking her exit, and all thoughts of jokes died away. She was trapped, and if the dragon breathed on her now she would be burned to a crisp. There was only one way out.

Grabbing the dragon's ears firmly with both hands, Cleo wedged her foot on the creature's slavering lower jaw and launched herself upward. The somersault wouldn't have won prizes for acrobatics, but it was straight enough to land her squarely on the dragon's neck. The beast roared in fury and raised up to its full height, flicking its head from side to side, but Cleo held firmly onto its scaly ears.

Resus finally managed to tip the egg over

the side of the nest and he struggled to catch his breath before jumping out after it. Across the cave he could see Luke stretching the Hex Hatch, while off to his left, Cleo appeared to be riding the dragon as though it was some kind of amusement park ride.

The creature reared up on its back legs, then slammed its front claws into the ground as it tried to dislodge the mummy. The whole cavern shook, knocking Luke off his feet and causing the egg to roll away from Resus's grasp. As the vampire dashed after it, he realized that this was the simplest way to move it. He pushed at the shell to keep the momentum going and tried to steer the egg in the direction of the Hex Hatch.

Luke jumped to his feet and plunged his hands back into the gradually widening window in the air, gripping the sides and pulling with all his strength. Glancing up, he could see Resus running toward him, rolling the egg across the bumpy floor of the cave. Meanwhile, Cleo was still clinging on to the dragon's ears as it swept its head around and bellowed in fury. If Luke didn't know better, he would have sworn he heard the mummy shout, "Yee-hah!"

Finally, the Hex Hatch was large enough for them to fit through. On the other side Luke could see a room unlike any he'd ever seen. It didn't, however, appear to have an angry dragon in it, and that was a serious plus. Luke sat on the bottom of the Hatch to bring it closer to the ground just as Resus arrived, bringing the egg to a shuddering stop.

"I can't say that's the easiest thing I've ever driven!" the vampire puffed.

Between them, the boys managed to lift the egg over the lip of the window and into the room on the other side. They laid the egg down and Luke stared around him. He ran his fingers through the deep pile of the carpet. There was something strange about it. "I . . . I think this carpet's made from hair," he said. "Human hair . . . "

Resus was busy fingering the leathery curtains hanging either side of the window. "That's skin!" he gulped. "And that coffee table is definitely made from leg bones!"

Luke swallowed. It was true. Everything in the room was constructed from human body parts, from the real arms at each end of the sofa

to the hollowed-out skull glowing softly at the top of the lamp in the corner. "Where are we?" he hissed.

"Little dudes!" bellowed a voice, making the boys jump. "To what do I owe the most awesome pleasure of your company?"

Luke spun around. A familiar—if rather rotten—figure was beaming at them from the doorway. "Doug!" he cried. "We *are* on Scream Street, then."

"Never a truer word spoken, wolf-man!" the zombie declared through decaying teeth. "Totally bodacious to see you, dudes. We thought we'd lost you for good!"

"You can't keep us away for long," said Resus, grinning.

"And you brought breakfast, too!" Doug drooled, and his moldy tongue ran over blistered lips as he eyed the dragon's egg.

"Sorry," said Luke. "This egg isn't for eating, I'm afraid. Resus, Cleo, and I need it to make a—"

"Cleo!" exclaimed Resus, suddenly remembering. The three of them peered back through the Hex Hatch to see Cleo still triumphantly

riding the dragon. She'd now tied a length of bandage around the creature's neck and was using it as reins.

"Man," whistled Doug appreciatively, "you dudes are awesome."

"Cleo!" yelled Luke, trying to make himself heard over the roar of the dragon. "Time to go!"

"Not until I've stopped her pain!" Cleo shouted back, letting go of the bandage reins and turning herself around. She slid down the dragon's scaly neck and across its back, and as she reached the tail, she stretched out and plucked the knife from the creature's belly. This caused the tail to flick up involuntarily, catapulting the mummy into the air and directly toward the open Hex Hatch.

"Look out!" cried Resus. "She's going to—"

Cleo flew straight through the Hex Hatch and landed squarely on top of all three of them, sending them crashing to the ground. One of the zombie's eyeballs popped out of his head as he hit the floor and was squashed under Resus's hand.

"Oh, I'm so sorry, Doug!" exclaimed Cleo, climbing off Luke's chest.

"No worries, little lady," the zombie assured

her, poking a diseased finger into the empty socket and feeling around. "I've got a drawer full of the things in the kitchen."

"It's me you should be apologizing to," groaned Resus, hastily wiping the goo off his palm. "This is disgusting."

"It was an accident," snapped Cleo. "I'm not going to apologize for—"

"Er . . . guys," interrupted Luke. "Can we argue about this later?" He gestured back toward the cavern, where the dragon, having spotted the Hex Hatch, was thundering toward them.

Luke pulled the paper back out of his pocket and found the place where he'd stopped reading. There was just one word left to say, and with any luck it would close the Hex Hatch. The dragon was almost upon them now, fire erupting from its gaping jaws. . . .

"*Unumbo!*" yelled Luke, and the window in the air disappeared just as the jet of flame burst into the living room. There was silence.

"Well," said Resus with a satisfied sigh. "That seems to have been a success!"

"Er, not entirely," said Cleo, tapping him on the shoulder.

81

Luke and Resus turned back toward the room to see Doug the zombie still standing where they had left him, burned to a crisp.

Chapter Ten
The Body

Luke's stomach churned for the third time as he watched Doug peel away the burned skin from his face, revealing a decomposing mess of muscle and bone beneath. He looked away and continued to scrape the top layer of shell from the dragon's egg, this time catching the dust in an old coffee jar.

Resus, on the other hand, was far from squeamish. He sat on a stool made from a human ribcage and watched the proceedings with fascination. "Can I have that?" he asked as Doug looked for somewhere to deposit the flap of charred flesh.

"One man's trash is another man's treasure," beamed Doug, handing it over.

"You're disgusting," groaned Cleo as Resus tucked the skin into his cape.

"I'm not!" retorted Resus. "You never know when something like that might come in handy."

Cleo shuddered. "I think I'm going to be sick," she moaned, turning away. But the view in the other direction wasn't much better. Doug's housemate, Berry, had her fingers pushed deep into a third zombie's skull.

"Duck snot!" cried the zombie.

"Don't worry about my man Turf." Doug smiled as he tore a strip of flesh from the sofa cushion and laid it across his own exposed cheek. "He's lost his mind."

"I wouldn't say he was that bad," said Cleo. "He's just a little confused."

"Instant boots!" bellowed Turf.

 84

"No, I mean he's *really* lost his mind—or some of it, at least," Doug continued, producing a staple gun from his pocket and using it to attach the new skin to his face. "It fell out of his head yesterday somewhere around the back of Everwell's Emporium. We'll go and look for it later—if we have time before the curfew."

Luke stopped scraping. "Curfew?"

"Yep—every night this week," explained Doug. "No residents allowed out after dark. Anyone caught out of their house after nightfall

will be escorted home by the Movers and placed under house arrest."

"Sir Otto Sneer's finally gone too far!" exclaimed Resus.

Doug shook his head, and as he did so his charred nose wobbled loosely. "Don't blame this one on the big man, little vampire. It's is all the work of that downer dude from G.H.O.U.L."

"Acrid Belcher," said Cleo.

"He's a bad man," said the zombie. "You should steer clear. I heard him tell the Movers to round up all the normals and take them to Sneer Hall."

The children exchanged concerned glances.

"What are we going to do?" asked Resus.

"I don't know," Luke admitted. "I wish I could ask Mr. Skipstone for advice."

"He's probably locked up in Sneer Hall as well," Cleo pointed out.

Doug ripped off his bottom lip and replaced it with another piece of skin torn from the sofa cushion. "They have the book man, too?"

Resus nodded. "Acrid Belcher confiscated *The G.H.O.U.L. Guide* before we were banished to the Underlands."

Doug sighed in dismay. "Totally bogus."

"Rubber peanuts!" Turf blurted out as Berry rummaged deeper inside his skull.

"What *are* you doing?" asked Cleo, a look of disgust on her face.

"Trying to work out which part of his brain is missing," the female zombie replied. "He seems to have all his movement . . ." She gave another prod and Turf's leg shot out, kicking Resus in the shin.

"Ow!" cried the vampire.

"Sorry!" said Berry. "I never was much good at brain surgery. Still, it's a very tasty hobby." She pulled her hand free and licked her fingers clean.

"We need to get the normals away from Sneer Hall and off of Scream Street," Cleo said to Luke and Resus. "I don't know what Sir Otto and Acrid Belcher want with them, but it can't be anything good."

"I agree," said Luke. "Then we close the doorway once and for all." He finished scraping the dragon's egg. "We bring Mr. Skipstone out of *The G.H.O.U.L. Guide*, make him transform into his werewolf, knock him out with

the sleeping potion, then stitch his claw back in place."

Resus couldn't help but smile. "You make it sound so easy."

"Is the sleeping potion ready?" asked Cleo, peering into the coffee jar.

"Almost," said Luke. "According to the recipe on the back of the map, I just have to mix this stuff with water." He turned to Resus. "Do you have any?"

The vampire produced a jug of water from under his cape and handed it over. "The potion isn't the part that's worrying me," he admitted.

Luke carefully poured some water into the coffee jar. "Then what is?" he asked.

"Saying good-bye to Mr. Skipstone."

"I've been thinking about that too," said Cleo. "*Skipstone's Tales of Scream Street* disintegrated as soon as we brought his spirit out of it. *The G.H.O.U.L. Guide* will do the same, won't it?"

"I'm pretty sure it will," said Luke ruefully.

"Plus, we haven't got another book to transfer his spirit back into after we return the claw," Cleo pointed out.

"Mr. Skipstone's going to die, isn't he," said Resus.

"Maybe," replied Luke. "But maybe not. . . ."

"What do you mean?"

"I've got this," he said, pulling what appeared to be a book from his pocket. It had a silver cover.

Cleo gasped. "That looks like . . ." She took it from Luke, but it was much lighter than she expected. Her face fell when she opened it up. "There's nothing in here. No pages at all."

"I took them out," Luke explained. "That used to be my dad's car manual. It's about the same size as *Skipstone's Tales of Scream Street*, so I cut the pages out and painted the cover silver."

Resus took the empty cover and examined it. "I'm not sure it will work," he said. "Even if it *looks* like Mr. Skipstone's book, I can't see his spirit rattling round between two bits of silver cardboard for all eternity."

"I've thought of that," Luke assured him. "We're going to get pages, written by Mr. Skipstone himself. He had tons of notes for his books in his house, remember? I reckon we can use his notes for *Skipstone's Tales of Scream Street*

to make a new copy of the book—or something pretty close to it."

"That's a great idea," said Cleo, "or at least it would be if all the notes hadn't gotten burned in a fire while we were trying to get the claw from him in the first place."

A smile spread across Luke's face. "Yes, but that's what happened to the notes *this* year," he said. "They're all still in one piece back in nineteen seventy-one."

Resus paled. "Oh, no," he said. "We're *not* going through my cape to nineteen seventy-one again. We almost killed Sir Otto last time."

"That wasn't us, that was the yeti," said Cleo. "Luke's right. If we ever want to see Mr. Skipstone's face on this, we have to go back in time to collect his notes."

Reluctantly, Resus unclipped his cape and stood beside his friends in the middle of the room. "I suppose so. Look after the egg, Doug: we'll be back soon."

A distant clock chimed midnight as Luke, Resus, and Cleo hurried across Scream Street's central square. Despite being in the year 1971, everything

looked the same—although they knew the sky would remain dark once dawn broke in a few hours' time.

The trip back through time via the cape had been uneventful, although they'd had to creep out of Alston Negative's closet without waking the sleeping vampire.

Resus produced a flashlight as they approached 1 Scream Street. "This shouldn't take too long," he said quietly, slipping one of his fake fingernails into the lock of the front door.

"You two start collecting the papers," hissed Cleo. "I'll be back in a minute."

"Where are you going?" asked Luke.

Cleo held the blue pendant up into the beam of the torch. "I want to return this to the empor-ium," she said. "I'll slip it under the door or something."

As she raced away, there was a soft click from the lock. "We're in," said Resus.

The boys crept into the darkened house and found their way to the author's study. There, sitting in his chair, was the body of Samuel Skipstone.

"If only we could wake him up now and take him back with us," said Resus.

 91

"It wouldn't work," Luke told him. "Then he wouldn't have been here for us to discover when we came back to collect the werewolf's claw in the future."

Resus frowned and rubbed his face. "Just thinking about this time travel stuff makes my head hurt," he groaned.

"Don't think about it, then." Luke smiled as he located the author's filing cabinet and slid open the first drawer. "Now, let's find the notes for *Skipstone's Tales of Scream Street* and get out of here."

"Dudes!" exclaimed Doug. "That looks just like the real thing!"

Luke glued the final page into the silver cover and examined his work. "I just hope it'll hold Mr. Skipstone's spirit after we've returned the final relic."

"I don't see why not," said Cleo. "That's his writing after all."

The mummy had arrived back from the emporium to find her friends rifling through vast piles of papers. Once they had found the right ones, they had quickly made their way back to Alston Negative's bedroom, and then home.

 92

"I still don't know how we're going to get a body," said Resus. "But we'll need one to bring him out of *The G.H.O.U.L. Guide*—when we finally get our hands on it. His own body crumbled to ashes, remember?"

Luke thought back to the moment when he, Resus, and Cleo had saved Samuel Skipstone's life by transferring his spirit into the pages of *The G.H.O.U.L. Guide*. Seconds later, the author's ancient body had crumbled away. "That's something I still haven't been able to figure out," he admitted.

"Can we dig up another body from somewhere?" asked Cleo.

"I'm afraid there aren't any corpses left in Scream Street," said Berry. "Not since that big barbecue we had back in the summer, anyway."

Doug grinned. "That was a righteous feast!"

Resus produced the bottle of reanimation gel and put it on the zombies' coffee table. "So what are we supposed to use this on?" he asked, staring into the sparkling liquid.

"Hang on," said Luke, grabbing the gel. "If we can make a new copy of Mr. Skipstone's *book*, then maybe. . . ."

He opened the bottle, tipped a tiny amount onto his hand, and rubbed it into the bones that made up the legs of the coffee table. They shimmered for a second then sprang into life, knocking Luke off his seat. The table then began to prance around the room like an excited puppy.

"Brilliant!" cried Cleo.

"I don't get it," said Resus.

Luke reached up and lifted the hollowed-out skull from the top of the lamp. "We're going to build ourselves an author!"

Chapter Eleven

The Normals

The body was almost complete. The trio had used the leg bones and feet from the zombies' sofa, the ribcage from the footstool, and arms snapped from the sides of Doug's bed to assemble something that looked human—almost.

Resus finished stapling one of the fleshy curtains around the frame in an attempt to give the figure some skin. "It looks like something a toddler would make!"

"What kind of toddler builds things out of body parts?" asked Cleo.

"I used to," replied Resus. "I even asked my mom and dad for a brain one Christmas. I didn't get it, though—just a pair of lungs. I was bummed."

"I am *so* glad I didn't know you then," Cleo said with a shudder.

"Speaking of brains, we'll need one for this thing to work," said Luke. He turned to Berry. "Are you sure Turf won't mind us borrowing what's left of his?"

The zombie plunged her hand back into Turf's skull to retrieve the lump of wobbly gray matter. "He won't even notice it's missing," she assured them.

Luke took it from her and dropped it into the empty head that had until recently housed nothing more than a lightbulb. "And we're finished!" he declared, clicking the skull into place at the top of the spine.

The trio stepped back to admire their handiwork.

"That," commented Cleo, "looks hideous."

"It doesn't matter what it looks like," Luke said. "It just matters that it works."

"There's only one way to find out," said Resus, reopening the bottle of reanimation gel. He emptied the gel into his friends' hands and the three of them began to rub it all over the make-shift body. After a moment, the figure began to sparkle, then it took a few tentative steps.

"Monkey nuggets," it announced.

"Well," said Cleo. "At least we know Turf's piece of brain is working. . . ."

"Let's hope it's enough to hold Mr. Skipstone for a while," said Resus.

Luke took the strange creature by the hand and led it toward the front door. "Are you sure you're happy to look after the dragon's egg while we're gone?" he asked Doug.

"No worries, little dude," the zombie assured him. "We'll keep this baby nice and cozy until you get back."

"OK," grinned Luke. "Let's go get Mr. Skipstone and save the normals."

"Save the normals!" repeated Resus. "I never thought I'd hear anyone say that."

"Spam hammers!" screeched the homemade body.

"Or that."

The body tottered comically down the garden path outside 28 Scream Street. "Stop!" commanded Luke.

The figure came to a halt. "Spider pee!" it shouted.

"What have you stopped it for?" asked Resus. "Aren't we going to Sneer Hall?"

"We are," Luke replied, "but don't forget that if we're seen, we'll be arrested again."

"Of course!" said Cleo. "We need to go in disguise. Who's got the gutweed?"

"Me," replied Resus, pulling the handful of stinking green fronds from his trouser pocket and handing it out. The three children each popped their share into their mouth and began to chew. In no time at all their shapeshifting abilities kicked in and they were able to change their identities once again.

"Gross!" exclaimed Cleo as Luke's skin began to decompose.

"*You're* not," said Luke as Cleo's own transformation was completed. He found himself struggling not to stare at her under the enchantment charm.

"It feels weird every time I do this," said Resus, peering down through his ribcage. He unclipped his cape and tucked it under a nearby bush.

"Candy feet!" barked the body.

"OK," said Luke, "so if anyone asks who we are, we're from another G.H.O.U.L. community, here to visit our relatives on Scream Street."

"Gotcha!" said Resus.

"Now, let's try to find a way into Sneer Hall."

The trio stepped out into the central square, the corpse at their heels. The place was swarming with Movers, and residents scurried by quietly with their heads down. The whole street was shrouded in a nervous, uneasy atmosphere.

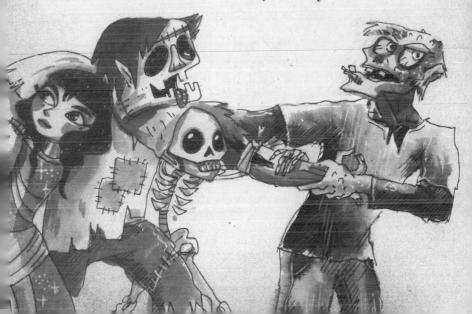

"Acrid Belcher's got his soldiers everywhere," hissed Cleo.

"But I can't see the nasty piece of work himself," Resus commented. "Or Sneer for that matter. Where do you think they are?"

"I don't know," Luke replied. "And that worries me. Stay sharp."

"Sheep burgers!" spat the body.

In the middle of the square, the doorway to Luke's world was now the size of a large doggie door. Anyone wanting to get through the orange portal would have to crawl on their hands and knees.

"I can't wait for that thing to be closed forever," said Resus.

"Not long now," Luke assured him. "We just need to make sure the normals are on the right side first."

Checking that no one was looking, the trio and their body buddy slipped through a gap in the fence around Sneer Hall and scurried toward the mansion. They pressed themselves up against the wall and peered into the nearest window. The room inside was dark, as were the next two.

"You'd think a couple of hundred tourists

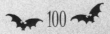

would be easy to find, wouldn't you," said Resus. "We should be able to hear them at least."

"Maybe it's time for Luke to use his werewolf ears?" suggested Cleo.

Luke nodded and closed his eyes. He thought about the way Acrid Belcher had made his parents watch as he had been plunged through the trapdoor into the Underlands, and he forced the feeling of anger up through his body and into his head. He felt his ears begin to stretch, and his nose began to lengthen into a snout.

"Oh, my Drac!" hissed Resus.

Cleo giggled.

Luke opened his eyes. Everything was tinted yellow now that he was looking at the world through his werewolf eyes, but that was perfectly normal. "What's the matter?" he asked. "You've seen me transform before."

"Yeah, but never quite like this," said Resus. "Check out your reflection. . . ."

Luke peered into one of the darkened windows and jumped in surprise. He'd transformed his entire head into that of a werewolf, just as he'd planned, but his usually sleek brown fur was rotting and clumped, and in places patches of gray,

diseased skin showed through. His ears were bent and twisted, and the tongue that lolled between his broken teeth was green and pockmarked.

He was a zombie werewolf!

"As long as I can still hear well, it doesn't really matter," said Luke. He pressed one of his huge, rotting wolf ears to the wall and listened carefully. "I can hear voices!" he exclaimed. "This way."

Luke led his friends around to the back of Sneer Hall, occasionally stopping to listen and check he was on the right path. Eventually he came to a halt at a plain wooden door. "I think they're in there," he said, allowing his features to return to those of a zombie.

Cleo tried the door handle. It was locked. "How will we get inside?"

"Leave that to me," said Resus.

Cleo looked at him questioningly. "How? You're not a vampire now, remember."

"Maybe not," smiled Resus, "but I still have this." He opened his hand to reveal one of his fake vampire nails, which he slipped over the end of a skeletal finger. He pushed it into the lock and

 102

began to twist it around, until—*click!*—he was able to swing the door open . . .

To reveal a huge cage completely filling the room beyond.

"I thought this was going too well," sighed Cleo.

"That's the cage Sneer kept my mom in when she first transformed," said Luke.

"Spy disco!" blurted the body.

"Wh-who's there?" came a quivering voice from the shadows of the cage.

Luke went over to the bars and found himself staring at a crowd of trembling normals.

"It's them!" cried another voice. "They're back!"

"What do you want with us?" pleaded a woman. "Why are you keeping us here?"

"Why won't you let us go?" demanded a man angrily.

"You don't understand," said Luke, "we're here to help."

"Don't trust him!" shouted the woman. "He's one of *them*!"

Cleo came to stand beside Luke. "He's not

 103

one of the Movers," she explained. "He's got a face—even if it is covered with scabs and sores."

"You're not with them?" asked the woman, edging forward.

The man grabbed her shoulder and pulled her back. "It's a trick!" he snapped. "They're all as bad as one another. We should never have come to this place."

"Finally, someone's said something I agree with," Resus muttered as he bent to peer at the lock on the front of the cage.

"What do you think?" Luke asked him. "Can you open it?"

Resus cracked his bony knuckles and took a deep breath. "Just you watch!"

Chapter Twelve
The Boy

Resus twisted his finger around inside the lock, wiggling the fake vampire nail until he heard a *click!* "One pin down, seven more to go," he grinned. "But it's a lot easier with these skinny skeleton fingers."

"Maybe you should keep them when all this is over," suggested Cleo. "Although you'd have to get used to the taste of gutweed."

"Keep working on the lock," said Luke, then he called to the crowd of normals inside the cage. "We're going to get you out of here. Out of Sneer Hall and off of Scream Street. But I need some help. Has anyone seen a golden book with a man's face on the cover? It's called *The G.H.O.U.L. Guide* and it's very important."

"I've seen that," answered a younger voice. A boy of around Luke's age stepped up to the bars. "It was in one of the rooms off the main corridor. I noticed it because for a moment it looked like the face on the front winked at me."

Luke gripped the bars of the cage, trying to hide his excitement. "Can you remember which room it was?"

"I . . . I'm not sure. . . ."

Cleo smiled at the boy. "My name's Cleo— what's yours?"

"Ethan," replied the boy. "I'm here with my cousin Arran and my uncle."

"These are my friends, Luke and Resus," said Cleo. "Could you show Luke where the book was if he took you back the way you came?"

The boy glanced timidly from Cleo to Luke and back again. "I think so . . ."

"There's just one problem," said Resus, not looking up from his work. "It's going to take me a while yet to get this lock open. He can't get out."

"Unless he squeezes through," suggested Cleo.

Luke looked thoughtfully at Ethan through the bars. He was slim—but was he slim enough?

"I can try. . . ." Ethan slid an arm and a leg between the thick metal bars and managed to get part of his body through, but then he couldn't get any further. "Sorry," he said.

"Don't apologize," said Cleo. "You almost did it."

"He did, didn't he," said Luke. "And I might be able to help him with that last little bit." Closing his eyes, Luke concentrated on transforming his hands into powerful werewolf paws. As before, the fur that burst through his skin was greasy, and weeping wounds erupted across his fingers as claws slid from their tips.

Once his arms had finished transforming, Luke gripped two of the bars with his paws and pulled. The metal creaked as the bars began to separate. "Quick!" he grunted. "Try now!"

Ethan squeezed himself between the bars and

found that he was now able to get all the way through and out of the cage.

"You did it!" cried Cleo.

"Come on," said Luke as his arms returned to normal. "Let's go."

"Good luck, Ethan!" called another boy from inside the cage. He was standing next to a man wearing glasses.

"That's Arran and his dad," Ethan explained.

"Will Ethan be safe with you?" asked the man.

Luke nodded. "If he can help us find the book, you'll all be safe." He turned to Cleo. "Try to convince the rest of them that we're not a threat."

"I'll give it a go," said Cleo. "Maybe the enchantment charm will help."

Resus reached into the cage and closed Arran's mouth as the boy stared in adoration at Cleo. "Trust me," he grinned. "It'll help!"

Luke took Ethan and the walking corpse around the outside of the mansion until they found an unlocked window. Luke cupped his hands together to give his new friend a boost up.

"I've only just escaped from this place," Ethan pointed out. "Are you sure we want to break back in?"

"We don't have a choice, I'm afraid," said Luke as Ethan pulled himself up onto the windowsill. "We need that book urgently." Ethan nodded and dropped out of sight. A few minutes later, a doorway swung open a little farther along the wall. Luke grabbed the corpse by the hand and led it inside.

The boys and the body crept along a corridor lined with suits of armor. "It was in one of these rooms, I think," whispered Ethan. "I remember seeing that painting." He pointed to a portrait of Count Negatov, Scream Street's vampire founding father and one of Resus's distant ancestors.

Luke smiled. The last time he had been in this particular corridor had been when he, Resus, and Cleo were trying to get their hands on the original *Skipstone's Tales of Scream Street.* "Can you remember which room?" he asked.

"That one over there, I think," replied Ethan, pointing.

Inside the room they found *The G.H.O.U.L. Guide* lying on Sir Otto's desk. The face protruding from the golden cover looked shocked as Luke approached. "Now, now," it warned. "You won't find any tasty organs inside me, I'm afraid! Just long words and complicated sentences."

"Mr. Skipstone!" interrupted Luke, snatching up the book. "It's me—Luke!"

"*Luke?*" inquired the author, squinting up through golden eyes. "Is it possible? I was told that all three of you had been banished to the Underlands!"

"We were," said Luke, "but we're back—and in disguise."

Skipstone smiled. "I thought I could detect the scent of gutweed!" He turned to Ethan and the body standing off to one side. "I must say," he said, "I would never have recognized Resus and Cleo, either."

"That's not them," Luke explained. "They're busy elsewhere. This is Ethan."

"Delighted to meet you, young man," said Skipstone. "And the other fellow?"

"That," declared Luke, "is the new you!"

Resus was still working on the lock when Luke, Ethan, and the body arrived back. Cleo hurried over to meet them. "Well?" she said. "Did you find it?"

"Thems did found it," muttered the corpse. "But me not happy chappy!"

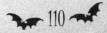 110

Luke couldn't help but smile. "Mr. Skipstone's struggling with the limited abilities of what's left of Turf's brain," he said. "He would have gone right back to *The G.H.O.U.L. Guide* if the book hadn't disintegrated the moment we transferred his spirit."

"Me hard time thinking," grumbled Skipstone. "Like swimming through snot."

"Oh, but it's still you!" exclaimed Cleo, throwing her arms around the strange figure. "It doesn't matter whether you can think or speak properly."

"It matter," said Samuel Skipstone crossly. "Me dumber than a box of toenails."

Click!

"That's the second-to-last one," announced Resus, wiping sweat from his brow.

Luke crouched down beside him. "How long do you think it will take to—"

The rest of his sentence was drowned out by the sound of marching feet, and he jumped up again. Quickly, he, Resus, Cleo, and Ethan ran outside, slamming the outer door after them and pulling Samuel Skipstone down behind a bush. They were just in time before several dozen Movers appeared, accompanied by Dixon.

 111

The landlord's nephew produced a bunch of keys and unlocked both doors, thankfully not noticing that the locks had been tampered with. "Come on, you all!" he called out to the normals. "Uncle Otto and Mr. Belcher want to see you in the square in fifteen minutes!"

Chapter Thirteen
The Square

Luke, Resus, Cleo, and Ethan watched from their hiding place as the Movers bound and gagged the normals, then led them away from Sneer Hall as though they were prisoners facing execution.

"Why would Sneer and Belcher treat the normals like that?" asked Cleo in disgust. "What do they want with them?"

"I've no idea," admitted Resus. "The normals can't line Sneer's pockets if they're tied up."

"Whatever it is, we'd better keep an eye on them," said Luke, climbing out from behind the bush. "Come on."

Resus took Samuel Skipstone's hand, and the five of them followed the group at a safe distance. By the time they reached the square, it was packed. The residents appeared to have also been summoned and were standing to one side in a nervous cluster, opposite the bound and gagged normals.

Movers took up positions around the edge of the crowd, each armed with a crossbow and sporting a belt lined with wooden stakes, silver spikes and metal bolts. They looked as if they were preparing to break up a riot.

"We should be able to mingle with the other residents without being recognized," whispered Luke, sidestepping around Mr. and Mrs. Crudley, their bog monster neighbors, and finding a space near the back of the crowd.

"But *I* can't mingle," Ethan said, paling. "You all look like you belong over here, but if they spot me I'll be tied up with the rest of the—what do you call us?—normals."

"He's got a point," said Cleo. "Do we have anything we can disguise him with?"

Resus shook his head. "I left my cloak back at the zombies' house."

"Bigger on the inside!" Skipstone blurted out, pointing to himself.

"Of course!" exclaimed Resus. He took hold of the sheet of leathery skin wrapped around the body and opened it far enough for Ethan to slip inside. "It won't be pleasant, but you should be safe."

Ethan made a face, then gave a quick grin before slipping through the opening at the front of the body and disappearing among the bones and organs inside. Resus smoothed the flap of skin back into place, hiding the boy from sight. "Perfect!" he grinned.

Cleo scanned the crowd. "Where are Belcher and Sneer?" she whispered.

"I don't know," said Luke, "but whatever they're planning, it's bound to be—"

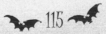

He froze, his eyes fixed on a couple at the other side of the crowd. His mom and dad.

"You OK?" asked Resus.

Luke nodded numbly. "They look like they haven't slept in days," he hissed. It was true. Mrs. Watson's eyes were bloodshot and swollen from crying.

"We haven't slept either," Resus reminded him. "They're just worried about you."

"I have to go and tell them I'm OK," said Luke fiercely, but Cleo put her hand on his arm.

"You can't," she said softly.

"Why not?" he demanded.

"Because they won't be able to stop themselves giving us away," she replied. "Then we can't help anyone at all."

"You're right," Luke said, sighing.

"Hang on," said Resus, "it looks like we're on. . . ." Sir Otto Sneer, Dixon, and Acrid Belcher had emerged from Everwell's Emporium, and the landlord's nephew was dragging a lectern behind him. He placed it in front of a microphone that had already been set up on a makeshift platform. When it was ready, Dixon stepped up to the

microphone and cleared his throat. Everyone in the square winced.

"Sorry!" gulped Dixon.

"Get on with it!" roared Sir Otto Sneer behind him.

Dixon nodded. "Uncle Otto has asked me to—"

"*Sir* Otto!" bellowed the landlord.

"Sorry!" squeaked Dixon. "*Sir* Uncle Otto has asked me to introduce a man who needs no introduction—so to be honest, I don't know why he's getting me to do this at all—"

"DIXON!"

"Er . . . the man who needs no introduction . . ." A look of horror flashed across Dixon's face. "What's his name again?" he asked in a stage whisper.

"You are a *moron*!" exploded Sneer.

"That's it!" beamed Dixon. "Please welcome U. R. A. Moron!"

There was a squeal as Sir Otto dragged his nephew away. Acrid Belcher took his place and surveyed the residents for a moment. Then he raised his swampy hands high in the air and gurgled, "I am your savior!"

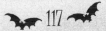

An unsettled murmur rippled across the square.

Acrid Belcher waited patiently for the noise to die down, then continued. "For centuries, unusual life-forms like you and me have cowered in fear—fear of being recognized for what we are, forced to leave our homes and sometimes even attacked for being different.

"Tortured and murdered, simply because we didn't look or act like *them*!" He thrust an accusing gloopy finger in the direction of the captured normals. "People just like these . . . these *normals*." He spat the word out. "*They* are the ones who have insisted that we're locked away from the rest of the world—moved to secure communities such as Scream Street, from which we cannot escape.

"For too long we have been expected to accept that living in purposely made neighborhoods was a good thing, for our own safety. But I stand before you today to say that *we* are the victims. This is not housing unusual life-forms for their own safety—this is imprisonment!"

Some of the residents began to applaud. Resus turned to Luke as they clapped. "He's got a point . . ."

Cleo punched his arm. "Don't you dare agree with anything he says," she hissed. "He's an evil maniac!"

Resus opened his mouth to reply, but Acrid Belcher's rasping voice was echoing around the square once more. "Let us not dwell upon the past, however," he gurgled. "Today I announce a new world order. A world where the normals are housed in sealed-off communities, and we—the unusual life-forms—are at liberty to roam the planet as free men, women, and monsters."

The slime beast fixed the residents of Scream Street with a steely glare, and proclaimed: "The world shall be ours and ours alone!"

Chapter Fourteen
The Children

The applause from the residents

was loud and long. Luke looked to see which of his neighbors was supporting this madman. The Crudleys, always eager to please those in authority, were slapping their muddy palms together enthusiastically, spraying those around them with clumps of muck and tendrils of thick, brown weed. Aside from them, two ogres, a gargoyle, and a family of imps appeared to approve of Belcher's plans.

"I foresee a world where vampires walk freely at night and get their blood from farms of free-range normals," the slime beast continued. "Bred especially to provide food for creatures of the night! Then their flesh can be pulped and used as feed for werewolves, pixies, and zombies. This is a world where wrongs will be righted. Where injustice will be fought. And where the 'freaks' will be in charge!" More applause echoed around the square as Belcher's hypnotic words took effect.

"OK," said Resus, "I was with him at the start, but this is getting weird."

"Pulped flesh?" exclaimed Cleo. *"Eurgh!"*

"I don't like this one bit," said Luke. "And it could get out of hand very quickly. We need to find somewhere for Mr. Skipstone to transform so that we can close the door at a moment's notice."

"That is smart, clever, top idea from your brain," confirmed Samuel Skipstone.

Luke waited until Acrid Belcher had started up again, then he gestured for Cleo, Resus, and Skipstone's temporary body to follow him. Out of sight of the swamp monster, the odd-looking group made their way to one of the yards that backed onto the square. Luke swung the gate open and gestured for his friends to follow. "OK," he whispered. "We shouldn't be spotted here."

"Don't come in—we're hiding!"

"You idiot! You've given us away!"

Luke spun around to see Resus's young cousin, Kian, crouching behind a hedge—and he wasn't alone. The other Scream Street children—Favel the banshee and the ghostly brothers Ryan and Finn Aire—were hiding behind a garden shed.

"What are you doing here?" Resus demanded.

"WE'RE NOT TELLING YOU!" screeched Favel. "YOU COULD BE WITH THAT HORRIBLE GREEN GUY FOR ALL WE KNOW!"

Resus glanced down at his skeletal body and sighed. "It's OK," he insisted. "It's me—Resus. And you'd better use your indoor voice, or we'll all be discovered!"

 122

Kian stood and glared at the skeleton. "Don't lie," he snapped. "My cousin Resus was banished to the Underpants."

"Underlands," corrected Ryan.

"Underlands," said Kian. "My aunt and uncle have been really upset—and if you pretend to be Resus, it will only make them sadder!"

Cleo crouched down beside the angry young vampire. "It *is* us, Kian," she said. "We're in disguise so that Acrid Belcher won't send us back to the Underlands."

"Cleo?" he gasped. "Is it really you?"

Cleo nodded. "I might look like a witch, but—"

"I'm a vampire!" declared Kian.

"You are," smiled Cleo, "and it's lovely to see you again."

"What's going on out there?" asked Ryan, pointing toward the square, where Acrid Belcher was still ranting, his squelchy voice getting louder and louder as the stunned residents and terrified normals listened in silence.

"It's just a madman planning on taking over the world," said Luke with a sigh.

"Nothing we can't handle," Resus added.

"Can I come out now?" asked a muffled voice. "It really smells in here."

"Ethan!" cried Resus. He pulled open the flap of skin at the front of Samuel Skipstone's body and allowed the boy to step out.

"Who is *that*?" asked Finn, staring up at the makeshift body.

"That's Samuel Skipstone," explained Cleo. "He's a genius. The cleverest expert on Scream Street there's ever been."

"I pee-peed in my pants!" said Skipstone.

Favel frowned. "Are you *sure*?"

Cleo nodded. "We've rescued his spirit from a golden book, and now we have to make him turn into a werewolf so we can sew this back in place." She produced a severed claw from her pocket.

"This place gets weirder every day," the banshee commented.

"OK," said Luke, turning to Samuel Skipstone. "Now we need you to transform, so I'm afraid we're going to have to make you angry."

Resus looked at the blank expression on Skipstone's face. He was starting to dribble. "That might not be so easy. . . ."

124

"What do you think would make you angry?" Cleo asked the author.

"Me not know," replied Skipstone. "Me find it hard to know anything in this brain."

"That could be it!" exclaimed Luke. "Mr. Skipstone, who was the original owner of Scream Street's emporium?"

"Er . . . me not know," came the grunted reply.

"OK, then, which founding father agreed to the building of Sneer Hall?"

"Me not know."

"Sorry to interrupt," said Resus, "but is this really the time for a Scream Street trivia quiz?"

"It's the perfect time," replied Luke. "Mr. Skipstone is used to having all his knowledge at his fingertips. Imagine taking that away from him. . . ."

"It would drive him crazy," said Cleo.

"Exactly!"

"Brilliant!" grinned Resus. "What's Nelly Twist's cat named?" he asked the author.

"Me not know," muttered Skipstone.

"How long did Dr. Skully work as a laboratory skeleton?" demanded Cleo.

"Me not know!" the corpse snapped.

 125

"Where did your son live after he escaped the clutches of G.H.O.U.L.?" asked Luke.

Samuel Skipstone's frustration was clear, even with the limited amount of muscle movement in his temporary face.

"ME NOT KNOW!" he growled, then he bent double, clutching at his open ribcage. Kian, Favel, and the Aire brothers jumped back in alarm.

Ethan stood rooted to the spot. "What's happening to him?"

"Let's hope he's changing into his werewolf. . . ." said Luke.

But this was nothing like Luke's own transformations. The bones and body parts activated by the reanimation gel simply fell apart onto the grass and began to reattach themselves in a new configuration.

The skull stretched to form a snout while vertebrae from Skipstone's spine connected up to form a bony tail. Fingers and toes snapped and reformed themselves as claws. Lastly, the sheet of leathery skin wrapped itself around the creature as a wrinkled, ageing hide.

Fully transformed, the werewolf raised its head to the sky and howled. . . .

Meowww!

The children remained silent. Then Resus cleared his throat. "Did he just say *meowww*?" he asked.

"Never mind that," said Cleo, producing the coffee jar. "Let's just get this in him." She unscrewed the top and tipped the contents onto the grass in front of the werewolf. The creature sniffed at the potion, then lapped it up hungrily. Within seconds, he was swaying woozily from side to side. Then, finally, he slumped to the ground and began to snore.

"Perfect!" exclaimed Resus. "And there's even a space on his paw for the missing claw."

"But we can't stitch it back on through bone," Cleo pointed out.

"I've got some glue," said Kian, plunging his hand into his cape. "I'm a vampire!"

"Wonderful," said Cleo as he handed her the pot of glue. "As soon as we've got the normals off of Scream Street we can reattach the claw. Then the doorway will close quickly behind them."

"I don't like leaving Mr. Skipstone alone here while we sort out the normals," said Luke. "What if he wakes up?"

"One of us could stand guard," suggested Resus.

"I can do that if you like," offered Favel.

"Thanks," said Cleo. "With any luck, we'll be back before too long."

"How are you going to get us out of here?" asked Ethan.

"I'm not sure yet," admitted Luke. "What we need is some kind of distraction."

The trio turned their attention back to what was happening in the square.

"But . . ." cried Acrid Belcher, "you might ask, who will be the ones to make my dreams a reality? Who will round up the normals and shepherd them into their new homes while we take our rightful places in the world?" He paused for

effect, his words echoing off the houses around the square. "And the answer is . . ." He turned to point a slimy, green finger back at the captive tourists. "YOU! *You* will become a new generation of Movers, destined to do my bidding and see in a new world order."

"*Ahem!*" coughed Sir Otto Sneer, standing on tiptoe beside the head of G.H.O.U.L. to be certain the assembled crowd could see him.

Acrid Belcher gestured for the landlord to step forward. "Of course, we have Sir Otto to thank for finding such a large number of 'volunteers.' And so . . ." The head of G.H.O.U.L. produced a thick wedge of banknotes, which he handed over to Sneer. The landlord accepted the money with glee and began to count it.

Luke gave a sharp intake of breath. "I think Sir Otto might have just sold the normals to Acrid Belcher."

"*Sold* them?" exclaimed Resus. "But they're not his to sell!"

"Maybe not," said Luke, "but Belcher's paid him for bringing them to Scream Street—and now he's going to turn them all into Movers."

"How will he do that?" asked Ethan.

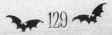 129

"Trust me," replied Resus, "you don't want to know."

"The operations will begin immediately," gurgled Belcher. "Take them away!"

Cleo watched in horror as the Movers began to herd the normals back toward Sneer Hall. "What can we do?" she cried.

Suddenly, an explosion sounded, rocking the entire street and knocking people to the ground. Acrid Belcher stopped in his tracks. The children looked around, trying to work out where the blast had come from.

Doug, Turf, and Berry's house, number 28, lay in ruins, and fire engulfed the pile of rubble that remained.

Then, through the flames, a shimmering blue shape appeared, screeching. A baby dragon. The creature unfolded its wings and took to the air with a loud cry.

Luke grinned. "I think we've just got our distraction."

Chapter Fifteen
The Blaze

Within seconds,
the whole of Scream Street was in chaos: residents
and normals alike ran screaming from the winged
beast. The dragon, equally scared, began to dive-
bomb the square, swooping low and breathing
fire at anything that moved.

Fences, trees, and soon entire houses were
quickly engulfed in flames. Whichever way the
residents turned, they were faced with a burning
building. Wherever the normals stumbled, a vast
and menacing shadow was headed their way.

"The baby dragon!" cried Cleo. "It's hatched!"

Resus rolled his eyes. "I see the brainiac's caught up."

Cleo grabbed him by his ribs. "The egg wasn't supposed to hatch," she retorted. "We were supposed to take it back to the mother's nest."

Resus pulled the mummy down just as a jet of flame shot out over their heads and exploded against the shed behind them, obliterating it. "We forgot to tell that to the egg," he quipped.

The dragon banked around, preparing to attack the square again. "But it'll be scared!" said Cleo.

More screams erupted as people fled, terrified, out of the creature's path. "Yep," said Resus. "It's definitely the dragon who's scared right now."

Luke turned to Kian. "Do you have anything in your cape that we can use to cut the rope around the normals' wrists?"

The young vampire began to rummage around inside his cloak. "I've got these," he said, producing a pair of plastic safety scissors.

"That's not exactly what I was thinking of . . ."

"How about these?" asked Ryan, floating across the lawn and snatching up a pair of

garden shears from the ruins of the shed. "There's another set of shears in here, and a couple of pairs of pruning scissors, too."

"Perfect," said Luke. "You, Ethan, Finn, and Kian—get out there and start freeing the normals. Cut the rope that's binding their wrists and tell them to make their way to the orange doorway and off of Scream Street as quickly as possible."

The ghostly brothers, Ethan, and the vampire grabbed their tools and ran for the gate. Cleo looked concerned. "Are you sure you want to do this?" she asked them.

Ryan beamed. "Are you kidding?" he said. "We've been watching you three have all the adventures—now it's our turn to join in!"

"This is the most exciting day of my life!" cried Ethan.

"We'll be careful," promised Finn.

"I'm a vampire," declared Kian.

"Favel," said Luke as the four of them disappeared out into the square, "let us know if the werewolf starts to come round."

"You got it!" said the banshee.

Luke turned back to Resus and Cleo. "Ready?" he asked.

Resus clapped a bony hand on each of his friends' shoulders. "Always!"

Cleo nodded. "Let's go."

The trio dashed back out onto Scream Street. Most of the houses that bordered the square were already in flames, and plumes of black smoke rose thickly from the side streets.

Luke spotted the orange arch of the doorway in the middle of the square and sprinted toward it. A thin trickle of freed normals had already gotten there, and they were now on their hands and knees, crawling back to their own world and safety.

"Go!" bellowed Luke. "Get out of here!"

A skeleton and a witch appeared beside him. "Half the normals are missing!" shouted Resus, trying to be heard over the screech of the baby dragon as it made another pass overhead. "There are loads more of them than this."

"They must be hiding somewhere!" Cleo yelled back.

"Search the yards!" cried Luke. "Take Finn or Ryan with you and get—"

Suddenly, Everwell's Emporium exploded, knocking the trio off their feet and showering the entire square with rubble and glass. Smoke billowed out of the store, and flickering flames could be seen as the stock inside caught alight.

"Was Eefa in there?" asked Luke, climbing back to his feet.

Cleo shook her head. "She's over there helping Kian," she replied, pointing to the far side of the square. Through the smoke, they could just about see the witch staring at what remained of her livelihood.

"There *is* someone inside, though," Resus said. "I can see movement. . . ."

As he spoke, Sir Otto Sneer, Dixon, and Acrid

Belcher emerged from the ruined emporium, coughing. Their clothes were in tatters and their faces black. "My street!" wailed Sir Otto, taking in the scene of devastation. "My beautiful street!"

"What are you moaning about?" demanded the swamp beast. "It's just bricks and mortar. I'm losing much more than that; I'm losing my dream."

"Nuts to your dream!" roared Sneer. "I'm not insured for any of this!"

"I gave you more than enough for the normals," gurgled Belcher.

Sir Otto paled as he remembered the money, and he began to fumble in the pocket of his waistcoat. After a few moments, he produced the charred remains of what had been a hefty wedge of banknotes. "NOOOO!" he sobbed, dropping to his knees and bursting into tears.

Luke took in the scene, thankful that the landlord and Acrid Belcher were too preoccupied with the damage to Scream Street to have noticed the normals escaping through the doorway. He, Resus, and Cleo continued to urge them on, keeping one eye on the sky in case the dragon came back.

 136

"I can't see it!" cried Cleo, gazing up into the smoke-filled air. "Where's it gone?"

A piercing screech off to the left caused Resus to clamp his bony hands to the sides of his skull. "Not far enough away by the sound of it!"

Luke grabbed the normals by their arms one after the other, helping them to slide through the low archway. "This way! Come on!"

The dragon's shadow darkened the square again. "Why are we just standing here and taking this?" Acrid Belcher demanded. He turned to the nearest Mover and pressed his slimy fingers to the man's forehead. "Open fire!" he gurgled.

The Mover raised his crossbow and fired. He missed the target, but the instruction quickly passed from Mover to Mover, and within seconds dozens more bolts and arrows were flying through the air. Some missed, but even those that were on target simply rebounded off the dragon's scaly hide.

Terrified by this onslaught, the dragon began to flit about, beating its wings hard and creating powerful gusts of wind that only helped to fan the flames of the burning buildings. Then it soared up and over Sneer Hall, spitting out a searing

 137

shaft of fire and igniting the upper story of the mansion.

"NOOOOOOOOOOOOO!" screamed Sir Otto as he watched his ancestral home begin to burn furiously. Dixon scuttled over and tried to calm his uncle by gently patting him on the head.

"Man up, Sneer!" thundered Belcher. "*I'm* the one losing out here—and I'll put a stop to it right now." Grabbing the crossbow from a nearby Mover, he followed the path of the dragon overhead, and fired.

This bolt didn't simply deflect off the dragon's dense skin. This one found its target, plunging between two scales and embedding itself deep into the creature's flesh. With a deafening screech, the dragon spun over onto its side and crashed to the ground.

Silence fell over Scream Street, and the only sounds to be heard were the crackle of the houses burning and the scratch of the dragon's long claws as it dragged itself across the ground, one wing held out away from its body. Thick, gloopy blood poured from the wound, giving the shimmering scales around it a dark purple hue.

 138

"There!" gurgled Belcher with delight. "That's how you take down a dragon!" He snatched another bolt from the Mover's hand and reloaded, but when he raised the bow again, he found something else in his sights. A young witch was making her way across the square toward the injured dragon.

"What are you doing?" hissed Resus.

"I can't stand by and let it suffer," Cleo called back. "I have to help it."

"It's dangerous!" cried Resus. "That thing has demolished half of Scream Street!"

But still Cleo advanced on the creature as it scratched limply about on the ground, plumes of black smoke pouring from its nostrils. "It's OK," she said softly, cautiously stepping up to the beast and running her hand over its scaly throat. "I won't hurt you."

The dragon pulled back slightly, but it seemed to sense that Cleo meant it no harm. Normals and residents watched nervously from around the square.

"I'm going to take that nasty bolt out now," Cleo told it calmly, sliding her hand toward the

wound. "It might sting a little, but I promise it will stop the pain. . . ." Then she grabbed the bolt and yanked it free.

The dragon let out another screech and pumped its wings, getting slowly to its feet. It padded forward, then launched itself into the air. Luke and Resus could barely watch as it circled back toward Cleo and began to dive — only to pull back up as it passed over her, eventually coming to land on the roof of one of the few undamaged houses. There it sat and began to clean the blood around the wound with its tongue.

Luke and Resus raced over to Cleo. "You did it!" cried Luke.

"I knew she would," declared Resus. "Didn't I just say she would?"

Then Mr. Crudley suddenly pointed a muddy finger in their direction and said, "I thought those children had been banished to the Underlands!"

Resus was the first to register. "Hey," he exclaimed, looking down at his fingers. "There's skin on my hands again."

"And the scabs and sores have all vanished from Luke's face," said Cleo, touching the bandages around her own eyes.

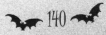 140

"It's the gutweed," said Luke. "It's worn off."

"YOU!" The trio spun around to see the head of G.H.O.U.L. throw down his empty crossbow and stomp toward them, leaving a trail of soggy footprints in his wake. "You've ruined everything—and now you're really going to pay!"

Chapter Sixteen
The Truth

"How did they get back?" cried Sir Otto.

"Have they been away?" asked Dixon blankly. "They might have sent a postcard!"

"It doesn't matter how they got back," snarled Belcher, slapping a gloopy palm against the skull of another Mover. "They'll never go anywhere ever again. . . ."

Within seconds, the trio was surrounded by Movers, all aiming their crossbows directly at them.

"Don't you dare!" came an indignant voice from across the square. Resus looked up to see his mom and dad racing toward them.

Luke's parents were just behind. "Stop!" cried Mr. Watson. "Luke!"

Niles Farr strode into Acrid Belcher's line of vision. "If you harm them, I will not be responsible for my actions," he warned.

"Stay back, freaks!" spat the swamp beast.

"There's only one freak around here," snapped Cleo, "and that's you!"

At this, Belcher raised his hand and slapped the mummy hard across the face, knocking her to the ground. Luke, Resus, and Niles all darted forward, but before they could reach the slime beast, the baby dragon, forgotten in all the excitement, let out a furious shriek and launched itself off the roof, its eyes fixed firmly on Belcher.

Luke and Resus grabbed Cleo by the hand, pulled her to her feet, and ran, closely followed

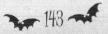

by their parents. The Movers, too, dropped their weapons and raced away, dodging around Dixon as he dragged Sir Otto to safety.

Alone in the middle of the square, Acrid Belcher stumbled backward away from the dragon, his swampy hands raised as it flew straight for him.

"N-no . . ." he glugged. "NO!"

A mighty flame erupted from the dragon's mouth—a flame that engulfed Belcher completely. When the smoke cleared, all that was left of the head of G.H.O.U.L. was a bubbling puddle of green liquid.

"Talk about melting under pressure," quipped Resus, seconds before his parents grabbed him in a bear hug.

"You're safe!" Bella Negative cried.

Mr. and Mrs. Watson did the same to Luke, hardly able to believe it was really him, and Niles Farr swept Cleo up into his powerful arms.

Luke finally disentangled himself from his parents' embrace. "I'll be back in a minute," he promised. "We need to do something first. . . ." He scanned the devastated square for the other children and spotted Kian. "We need to get the

144

rest of the normals out of here," he said. "Can you help?"

"Of course," smiled Kian. "I'm a vampire!" He skipped into the middle of the square and shouted, "Hey, normals—this way!" Then he leaped into the air, whipped his cloak around himself, and turned into a tiny bat.

One by one, the normals emerged cautiously from their hiding places. Ryan and Finn dashed among them, cutting the ropes around their wrists and pointing to where Kian hovered above the small orange doorway out of Scream Street. Soon, their neighbors were hurrying over to help—Dr. Skully, Eefa Everwell, Doug and Berry, Twinkle, the Crudleys, and even Dixon.

Luke, Resus, and Cleo stood by the doorway, wishing everyone well as they crawled back to their own world. Finally, only three normals remained: Ethan, his uncle, and his cousin, Arrun.

"You kept Ethan safe," said his uncle, shaking each of them by the hand. "Thank you so much."

"It was nothing," said Resus. "We do this sort of thing all the time!"

Arran and his dad crawled through the doorway, leaving Ethan alone with his new friends. "I guess I won't see you guys again," he said.

"I don't suppose so," said Luke. "But make sure you don't forget us!"

"Who could ever forget Scream Street?" Ethan grinned. Then he was gone.

"Right," said Luke to Resus and Cleo. "Let's do it." The trio raced across the square and into the yard where Favel was still watching over Samuel Skipstone's werewolf. Luke took the glue and the claw from the banshee.

"Ready?" he asked.

"Ready!" said Resus and Cleo together.

Resus held the pot while Luke smeared glue over the length of bone that stuck out from the claw. Then he pressed the relic back into place on the sleeping werewolf's paw.

Instantly, there was a burst of orange light above the square.

"Come on!" yelled Resus, dashing for the gate. The trio ran back into the square just as the final section of the doorway to Luke's world exploded in a shower of orange sparks and disappeared, sealing Scream Street off forever.

"Well," said Luke, "we did it!"

"I was never in any doubt," said Resus.

"Simple," said Cleo.

"We knew you could do it!" cheered Mrs. Watson, and Alston Negative gave his son a proud pat on the back.

However, their celebrations were interrupted by a slow handclap. "Oh, how touching." Sir Otto Sneer, a fresh cigar jammed between his teeth, was sauntering over. "So, you've closed the doorway and saved Scream Street—no, make that the world!—from the slimy green madman. And now we can begin to rebuild the houses and start life anew."

"What do you want, Sneer?" Luke asked warily.

"What do I *want*?" Sir Otto growled. "Where should I start? You've cost me *everything*! The money I earned from allowing normals to tour this place, the cash Belcher gave me so he could turn them into Movers . . ."

Behind the landlord, as if to punctuate his words, the upper story of Sneer Hall collapsed onto the already burning ground floor. "*And* my home!"

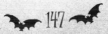

147

"That wasn't us," cried Cleo. "That was the dragon!" She gestured to the majestic creature, now sitting calmly among the ashes of Everwell's Emporium. "And plenty of other people lost their homes today too," she added.

"All thanks to you three," growled Sir Otto.

"I don't think so," snapped Resus. "If *you* hadn't started bringing normals to visit Scream Street, none of this would have happened."

"He's right," said Tibia Skully bravely. "It *is* Sir Otto's fault!"

"It was Sneer wot caused all this," agreed Twinkle.

"The dude has been messing with our karma for years, man!" added Doug.

Sir Otto looked up to see the residents of Scream Street all gathering around and fixing him with angry glares. Luke grinned at Resus and Cleo. "They're standing up to him!" he hissed.

"You've treated us like animals!" shouted Bella Negative.

"Worse than animals!" yelled Molly Aire.

"Stay back!" Sneer barked. "You don't know what I'm capable of . . ."

"Er . . . Uncle Otto?" interrupted Dixon,

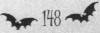

scampering up to the landlord. "I don't think this is a good time to upset people."

"You imbecile!" roared Sneer. "It's *always* a good time to upset people. A firm hand is the only thing these freaks understand."

"I think you could be underestimating them," came a distant voice. Sir Otto jumped as a Hex Hatch sprang open in front of him. Zeal Chillchase clambered through, accompanied by Icus. As the pair stepped onto Scream Street, a furious leprechaun flung itself at the Tracker, pulling his hair and biting at his ear.

"Get back to Dead End, Rooney!" roared Chillchase, tearing the struggling leprechaun from his head and hurling him back through the window in the air. Icus quickly muttered a spell and the portal snapped closed. "Now . . ." said the Tracker, smoothing down his long leather coat. "Where will I find Acrid Belcher?"

"Er . . . you're standing in him," said Resus.

Chillchase looked down at the green puddle on the ground. "*That's* Belcher?"

"It was *them*!" said Sneer, pointing an accusing finger at the trio. "They brought a dragon here and murdered Acrid Belcher."

"A dragon?" asked Icus, scanning the square until she spotted the creature among the ruins of the emporium. She threw her head back and screeched.

"That sounds just like the dragon's cry!" exclaimed Cleo.

"Hardly surprising," said Chillchase. "She is half dragon after all."

The creature responded with a screech of its own, then it took to the air.

"It's not going to start burning things again, is it?" asked Luke.

"Not at all," said Icus. "I just asked the little fellow where he lived."

"It's a boy?" asked Cleo.

Icus nodded. "And a very handsome boy at that! Now, I think it's time to send him home. . . ." She began to mutter a spell, and the largest Hex Hatch the trio had ever seen opened in the sky above Scream Street. On the other side, Luke, Resus, and Cleo could just make out the cave where they had first found the egg, together with the head and neck of the mother dragon. With a final shriek, the baby flew through and the portal snapped shut behind it.

"Done!" said Icus.

"It most definitely is *not* done," barked Sir Otto. "I want to know what punishment G.H.O.U.L. will be handing down to these three troublemakers."

Zeal Chillchase pondered Sneer's words for a moment before answering. "As G.H.O.U.L.'s head Tracker," he said, "I was second in command to Acrid Belcher. I must therefore assume his duties now that he has left us." He pulled a handkerchief from his pocket and wiped the green goo from his boots.

"WHAT?" spat Sneer. "He was your superior!"

"He was evil," insisted Icus.

"He wanted to turn the normals into Movers!" Twinkle the fairy pointed out.

"And lock the rest of the world away so people like us could rule," added Mr. Crudley. "Not that I agreed with any of that nonsense, of course . . ."

Chillchase removed his mirrored sunglasses and fixed Sir Otto with a hard stare. "It appears that you are in the minority when it comes to your appreciation of Belcher's plans," he said.

There was a crash behind them as the last

section of Sneer Hall succumbed to the flames. "Sir Uncle Otto," peeped Dixon, "I think the fire's reached the wine cellars. . . ."

Everyone turned to watch as the remainder of the landlord's ancestral home collapsed in on itself.

"He'll be *whining* about that next," quipped Alston Negative.

"Never mind, Sir Otto," said Berry. "You can stay in our spare room until you find somewhere else. We'd love to have you for dinner!"

"I'd be careful if I were you," commented a gargoyle. "I bet he'd give you terrible indigestion."

A ripple of laughter spread through the crowd.

"That's it!" rumbled Sneer. "It's finally time to teach you freaks some respect!" The landlord closed his eyes and gave a bizarre, animal snarl. Then, strangely, his body began to change. The crowd looked on, open-mouthed, as the land- lord's bones snapped noisily and he began to grow.

"What's happening?" exclaimed Mr. Watson.

Sir Otto roared as his muscles tore apart, knit- ting back together in stronger configurations. And

still he continued to expand, becoming taller and wider by the second.

"He's—he's transforming!" cried Luke. It was true: Sneer's face was beginning to twist and contort, the skin stretching outward.

"He can't be," said Resus, unable to tear away his gaze.

"He is!" exclaimed Cleo. "After all these years of calling us freaks, he's just the same. He's one of us!"

Chapter Seventeen
The Battle

Sir Otto yelled in pain as the bones in his hands snapped and fused back together, the nails spreading to coat the stumps and form thick hooves. The leather of his shoes burst open as his feet did the same. Coarse, brown fur sprouted all over his body and his hair flopped out in a long mane down his back while his ears slid up to sit at the top of his head.

By now he towered over the crowd, and they looked like toys beside him. The landlord opened his mouth and roared, and as he did so his teeth lengthened and twisted into two vicious tusks. The white scarf fell away from his throat, revealing the ragged mess of torn skin hidden beneath.

"Wh-what is he?" stammered Cleo.

"I don't know," replied Luke.

"I think I do. . . ." said Resus with a gulp.

Sir Otto growled deeply and glared down at the trio. Luke could feel the sound reverberating in his stomach. Then the landlord gnashed his teeth, his thick tongue flicking around until the growls began to sound like words.

"This . . . is your . . . fault," he rumbled.

"He can speak!" cried Resus.

"This is . . . YOUR FAULT!" bellowed Sneer.

"Of course it isn't," Cleo retorted bravely.

The warthog snorted, the flaps of skin at its throat vibrating. "You made me this!" it growled.

"We had no choice!" shouted Resus. "You lost a lot of blood when the yeti attacked you. Cuffy sent me to find a bottle of animal's blood to replace what you'd lost, and I chose . . . I chose warthog."

"WHY?" thundered Sir Otto. "WHY WARTHOG?"

"It was the biggest bottle there!" protested Resus. "I wanted to be sure Cuffy had enough to help you."

"You made me a MONSTER!"

"You've spent years making life as miserable as possible for the people who live here," said Luke incredulously, "yet all along you knew you were no different. Maybe you're right. Maybe you *are* a monster."

Resus watched thick tendrils of drool drip from the warthog's mouth. "Still," he said, "at least we didn't make him any uglier."

With a bellow of rage, the warthog sprang forward and dipped its head. Catching Resus with one of its tusks, it tossed him across the square.

"Stop it!" yelled Cleo. "You can't—"

A heavy hoof caught her in the side of the head and knocked her to the ground.

"I'm warning you," snarled Luke. "You're making me angry."

"That's the idea!" boomed Sir Otto. "It'll be so much more satisfying to squash you when you're in your little doggy costume!"

Luke's own transformation happened almost instantaneously, and for once he almost reveled in the pain of his twisting bones and tearing muscles. As his snout lengthened and sharp teeth pushed out through his gums, he tossed his head back.

HOOOOOOOOWWWWLLLL!

The crowd watched in terror as the two creatures began to circle each other in the center of the square. Luke's dad went to step in, but Zeal Chillchase stopped him. "Stay out of the way," he ordered.

Luke's werewolf bared its teeth and growled at the beast towering over it.

"Time to die, mongrel!" thundered the warthog, raising its front hooves and bringing them smashing down toward the werewolf. But Luke's werewolf deftly rolled out of the way and the thick hooves crashed onto the concrete.

Luke flipped over and lashed out with a paw, ripping at Sir Otto's throat with his claws. The warthog roared with pain and flicked its head to the side, catching Luke's injured knee with its tusk and ripping the stitches open.

Luke's werewolf fell to the ground with a

yelp, blood running down its leg and soaking into its thick fur.

"Time to finish this!" hollered Sir Otto's warthog, raising its hooves once more. The werewolf tried to drag itself clear, but it couldn't quite . . .

Then a flash of blond fur shot past as a second werewolf pounced, sinking its teeth into one of Sir Otto's front legs and sending them both tumbling backward.

"It's Luke's mom!" cried Cleo.

The warthog's head smashed against the ground with a sickening thud, and the creature lay there for a moment, stunned—just long enough for Luke's mom's werewolf to spin around and bare its teeth, ready to strike at Sir Otto's throat.

But the warthog was faster. As the blond werewolf lunged forward, Sir Otto caught its flank between his own massive teeth and bit down hard. The warthog shook the wolf around like a ragdoll, eventually tossing it into the ruins of the emporium. Then it turned back to Luke, who was still lying in a pool of blood.

"Stay away from him!" shouted Mr. Watson, racing across the square to protect his son. Sir

Otto gave a snort and knocked him aside with his hoof, cutting a deep gash into his cheek and sending him sprawling. Cleo dashed over to help him, tearing a strip of bandage from her side to press onto his face.

The warthog raised itself to its full height and gave a deep, otherworldly laugh. "Is there no one in your family who can stand up to me?" it demanded.

As if in answer, a third werewolf leaped over a nearby hedge and landed at the warthog's feet. This one was barely a skeleton, wrapped in a sheet of shriveled, leathery skin. Clumps of rotting fur clung to its frame and a diseased tongue hung limply between two rows of yellowing teeth.

"Mr. Skipstone!" cried Resus.

"Of course!" roared the warthog. "It finally makes sense. You're all related!"

Samuel Skipstone advanced on the warthog, snarling. Sir Otto stood his ground, then he saw Mrs. Watson's wolf crawl out of the rubble of the emporium and join her ancestor. Lastly, Luke forced himself to stand, gritting his teeth against the pain, and limped toward the warthog.

 159

Sir Otto's eyes flicked from one werewolf to the other as the three of them slunk toward him, snarling. The warthog opened its mouth and let out a terrifying roar, but it couldn't disguise its fear. It began to back away, then it reached the curb and tripped, crashing down onto its back.

It twisted its head from side to side to keep the three werewolves in its sight, and one by one they lifted their snouts and howled.

*HOOOOOOOOWWWWWLLLLL!
HOOOOOOOOWWWWWWLLLLLLL!
MEEEEEEEOOOOOOWWWWWW!*

The three werewolves were now standing over Sir Otto's warthog—it could feel their hot breath against its thick hide—and it began to transform back to human form. Its tusks pulled back into its mouth, the hair disappeared, and it shrank back to Sir Otto's usual rotund shape.

"You see what they're like," the landlord yelled to Zeal Chillchase, his voice quivering. "They're a dangerous family. They attacked me! You should send the whole lot of them to the Underlands."

Chillchase strode over and the wolves parted to allow him through. "From what I saw, they acted in self-defense," he said.

"That's right!" shouted Resus. "*He* transformed first."

"I lost my temper, that's all," said Sir Otto, beginning to whine. "I've never transformed properly—I've managed to keep it under control ever since I was a child. It's not my fault!"

Chillchase grabbed the landlord's arm and

dragged him to his feet. "It was your fault, however, that you attacked a normal."

"*What?*"

Zeal pointed to where Cleo was tending the cut on Luke's dad's cheek. Then he pulled his mirrored sunglasses from his pocket and slipped them back on. "Of course, you of all people should know the punishment for an unusual life-form who attacks a normal. It's exactly what brought Luke's family here, after all."

Sir Otto stared at the Tracker in terror. "No!" he begged. "No—please don't!"

Chillchase approached the nearest Mover and pressed his fingertips against his forehead. "Move Sir Otto to a new G.H.O.U.L. community so that he can live among his own kind and learn to control his transformations," he instructed. Two more Movers gripped the landlord by the arms, dragging him toward the edge of the square.

"NO!" screamed Sir Otto. "You can't do this! I'm not a freak! I'm Sir Otto Sneer!"

A thin, red-haired man pushed his way out of the crowd and dashed after the landlord as a Hex Hatch opened and the Movers began to pull him through. "Don't forget me, Uncle Otto!" yelled

Dixon, diving through after them. "I won't let them move you by yourself. I'll come and keep you company!"

Sir Otto's screams echoed around the square long after the Hex Hatch had closed, and he and his nephew were lost from sight.

Slowly, Luke and his mom began to transform back to their human forms.

"I can't believe it!" beamed the mummy, racing over and taking Luke's paw as it changed back into his own hand again. "Sneer's gone!"

Resus grinned. "Just like him to *hog* the limelight on the way out."

And one by one, the residents of Scream Street began to applaud.

Chapter Eighteen
The Future

It took almost two days for the fires around Scream Street to be put out and for the rebuilding work to begin. By the time the residents gathered in the square again, Movers were already erecting scaffolding around the damaged houses and had started to dig the foundations for what would become the new Everwell's Emporium.

This was the second time in the past few days that the residents had been summoned to the square, but this time the atmosphere was very different. Friends and neighbors chatted happily, eagerly awaiting the arrival of Zeal Chillchase, who was now officially confirmed as the new head of G.H.O.U.L.

Luke, Resus, and Cleo ambled through the crowd to where Eefa Everwell was watching the Movers work on her shop. "How's it coming along?" asked Cleo.

"Slowly," replied Eefa, but she smiled. "I offered to speed things up with a little magic, but the Movers didn't seem interested."

"Don't worry," said Twinkle, coming down to land beside the group. He winked at Eefa. "We'll sneak back here wiv our wands after they've clocked off and give the work a bit of a boost!"

"It can't be too soon for me, fairy dude!" said Doug, limping over. "I got me a serious case of the munchies—and Turf here needs a new lower intestine."

"Turf!" cried Resus as the other two zombies came to join them. "Did you manage to find the rest of your brain?"

"I'm afraid not," said Berry. "But I think he'll be OK without it."

"Surfer boogers!" bellowed Turf.

"Luke Watson!" called a stern voice. The trio turned to see Dr. Skully approaching, the other children scurrying after him with exercise books in their hands. His skeletal dog, Scapula, bounded along behind.

"I'm a vampire," announced Kian.

"I appreciate that you three have been through something of a trial," said the skeletal teacher, "and that Luke's injured leg may excuse him from gym class for a while. But I expect all of you back in class first thing on Monday morning!"

"Yes, sir," said Luke.

"Splendid!" replied Dr. Skully, leading the group to a spot at the front of the square. "Now, come along, children—I want you to take notes

on whatever Mr. Chillchase has to say and write a three-thousand-word essay on his major themes."

"Typical," groaned Resus as soon as the teacher was out of earshot. "We save the street, and we still have to go to school."

"I should think so!" came a voice from Luke's pocket. Luke pulled out the copy of *Skipstone's Tales of Scream Street* and turned it over to reveal the author's face protruding from the silver front cover. "A good, solid education is incredibly important," continued the author.

"And incredibly boring," mumbled Resus.

"How are you doing in there, Mr. Skipstone?" asked Cleo.

"Oh, I'm absolutely fine, young lady," beamed Samuel Skipstone. "Much better than I was inside that body you built for me—not that I'm ungrateful, of course."

"Of course," smiled Luke.

"But that tiny portion of zombie brain was so constricting," said the author. "Now that I'm back inside the pages of my research, I have room to think again."

As Skipstone finished speaking, a Hex Hatch appeared by the gates to the ruined Sneer Hall,

and Zeal Chillchase stepped through. Luke, Resus, and Cleo hurried over to where the other residents were already gathered.

Chillchase waited until everyone was silent before speaking. "A new era has begun at G.H.O.U.L.," he announced. "A time for righting wrongs and correcting the mistakes of the past."

"I wish it was a time for banning school," grumbled Resus under his breath.

"Ssh!" hissed Cleo, elbowing him in the side.

"But that is for the future," said Chillchase, "and I'm here to talk about today." A murmur of anticipation spread through the crowd.

"For generations, Scream Street has belonged to the Sneer family. However, as a result of recent events, the current owner has been removed from our midst."

"Where *is* Sneer now?" gurgled Mrs. Crudley.

"Sir Otto currently resides in a G.H.O.U.L. community in South America that consists mainly of canvas tents and a multitude of insects," said Chillchase, resisting the urge to smile as the entire square erupted in applause.

"This leaves G.H.O.U.L. in something of an unusual position," he continued. "We must

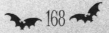

answer the question of Scream Street's future. Like most of you here today, Sneer had to surrender ownership of his home when he was moved."

"So he's lost Sneer Hall," said Volt Aire. "What's that got to do with the rest of us?"

"Otto didn't just own the mansion," Zeal reminded the crowd. "The whole street belongs to him. And G.H.O.U.L. cannot look after a community without the permission of the landlord. So, ordinarily, Scream Street would pass into new hands. . . ."

A ripple of excitement ran through the crowd. Mr. and Mrs. Crudley clasped their gloopy hands together tightly. "Please let it be us! Please let it be us!"

Doug took a swig from his bottle of saliva and beamed. "Dudes!" he proclaimed "If I get Scream Street, the party's at my place! 'Cause it'll *all* be my place!"

"Don't be ridiculous," barked Mrs. Crudley. "Who'd trust you with an entire street? No, Scream Street should belong to someone intelligent and organized."

"I couldn't agree more," said Dr. Skully,

puffing out his ribcage and crossing his bony fingers behind his back.

Zeal Chillchase waited until the crowd became quiet once more. "There are, of course, several other members of the Sneer family— including his nephew, Dixon and sister, Queenie. However, neither of these individuals is judged to be a suitable replacement landlord."

"I should think not," Resus whispered loudly. "One's about as sharp as a sack of wet rats and the other's a psycho!"

Luke and Cleo stifled their giggles.

"And so," said Chillchase, "the difficult decision has been made to allow Sir Otto to return to Scream Street . . ." Zeal ignored the gasp from the crowd and continued, "after a year in the jungle learning how to control his transformations."

"Sneer's coming back?" groaned Berry.

"Yes, but we get twelve months without him," Alston Negative pointed out. "A whole year to put things right before we see his ugly mug again."

"What happens in the meantime?" asked Eefa. "Who looks after Scream Street until then?"

"We are in the process of interviewing caretaker landlords," Zeal replied.

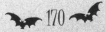

"There's no need," cried Tibia Skully. "We have the perfect candidates right here—Luke, Resus, and Cleo!"

The trio jumped at the sound of their names. "What?" exclaimed Resus.

"She can't mean it," hissed Cleo.

"Tibia's right," said Twinkle. "Them three have done loads for Scream Street. They should be in charge."

"I AGREE!" screeched Favel's banshee grandmother.

"I think they *do* mean it," Luke whispered in amazement.

Zeal Chillchase paused for a moment, and the crowd waited with bated breath for his decision. Finally, he pulled off his sunglasses and smiled. "If that's what you want, then the temporary landlords of Scream Street will be Cleo Farr, Resus Negative, and Luke Watson."

"Hooray for Luke, Resus, and Cleo!" Kian piped up.

The crowd laughed and erupted in cheers and applause.

Resus turned, wide-eyed, to Luke and Cleo. "We *own* Scream Street for a year?"

 171

Before either of them could reply, the trio were dragged out to the front of the crowd. Zeal Chillchase produced three scrolls from the pocket of his coat and handed one to each of them. "Sign these, and you're the temporary owners of Scream Street!"

"Congratulations!" cried an excited voice. Luke pulled *Skipstone's Tales of Scream Street* from his pocket to see the author beaming excitedly up at him. "I always knew you'd make this place great again!"

Luke looked from smiling face to smiling face as the applause continued. He spotted his parents watching proudly and gave them a quick wave. Niles Farr was laughing and crying at the same time, tears of joy soaking into his bandages. Even Mr. and Mrs. Crudley appeared to be smiling.

"I don't know what to say," Luke admitted.

"Neither do I," agreed Cleo. "Apart from thank you, of course!"

Resus waved his scroll in the air. "Hey—does this mean I can ban school?" he asked.

"No, young man, it does not," replied Dr. Skully. "And don't expect any special treatment just because you temporarily own a third of the classroom!"

Resus grinned. "Worth a try . . ."

As the residents laughed, Scapula dashed past, a gray, slimy lump wedged between his bony jaws.

"Hey," said Cleo, "is that what I think it is?"

"Yep." Luke laughed. "Scapula's found the rest of Turf's brain!"

"Come back here!" yelled Resus.

And the three friends chased the skeletal dog across the square and down Scream Street. . . .

Then the ground in front of them began to split open. The cracks spread like a spiderweb, moving at lightning speed and growing wider by the second.

Luke grabbed Resus and pulled him back before his foot slipped down one of the cracks. "What's going on?" he asked in amazement.

"Your guess is as good as mine!" replied Resus.

"Whatever it is, I don't like the look of it. . . ." said Cleo.

There was a sound like crashing thunder and one of the cracks opened wider than the others. A head appeared: a vast, swollen head with bulbous eyes, a nose the size of an armchair, and a gaping, wet mouth.

"Is that . . . Is that a *giant*?" exclaimed Cleo.

"Whatever it is, it's certainly been eating all its vegetables," remarked Resus.

Gargantuan fingers slammed down onto the ground as the giant began to climb out of the hole. "DESTROY!" it roared, shaking the whole of the street with its booming voice. "SMASH! DEMOLISH! OBLITERATE!"

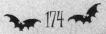

Resus pulled a cricket bat, a golf club, and a flaming torch from his cape and handed them out to his friends.

Luke gripped the handle of the bat tightly and cracked his neck from side to side. "Here we go again. . . ."

Have YOU read them all?

Meet Luke Watson: reluctant werewolf and Scream Street's latest arrival.

Scream Street has been invaded—by vampire rats.

3 — Scream Street just got darker.

4

The zombies have arrived
on Scream Street.

"Exactly the sort of grisly, gross, and hilarious stuff
that kids will love!" —Eoin Colfer, author of *Artemis Fowl*

TOMMY DONBAVAND

SCREAM STREET
FLESH OF THE ZOMBIE

Free collectors' cards inside!

"Exactly the sort of grisly, gross, and hilarious stuff
that kids will love!" —Eoin Colfer, author of *Artemis Fowl*

TOMMY DONBAVAND

SCREAM STREET
SKULL OF THE SKELETON

Free collectors' cards inside!

5

There's a monster loose
on Scream Street.

6

Scream Street is
full of surprises.

"Exactly the sort of grisly, gross, and hilarious stuff
that kids will love!" —Eoin Colfer, author of *Artemis Fowl*

TOMMY DONBAVAND

SCREAM STREET
CLAW OF THE WEREWOLF

Free collectors' cards inside!

7

Scream Street is being invaded.

8

Trolls: they're big, they're ugly . . . and they're always hungry!

9

The Nightwatchman: striking fear into all.

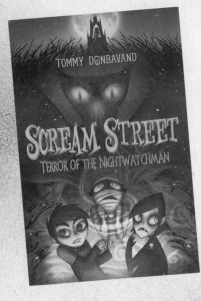